A Way to Catch the Dust

A Way to Catch the Dust

SHORT STORIES

by

Jacob Ross

Mango Publishing

1999

© Jacob Ross and Mango Publishing 1999

First published 1999

Published by Mango Publishing, London UK
P.O. Box 13378, London SE27 OZN

ISBN 1 902294 08 4

British Library Cataloguing in Publication Data
A CIP catalogue record for this book is available from the British Library

Printed in the UK by Watkiss Studios Ltd, Biggleswade

Cover photograph and cover design by Jacob Ross

Contents

Acknowledgments

This collection would have remained no more than an idea had it not been for the support, feedback and persistence of Joan Anim-Addo. This book is as much hers as it is mine.

Language does not allow me to express the importance of the following people in my writing life: Pauline Cohen, Judith Lockhart, Manisha Amin, Bernardine Evaristo, Janet Jam Tsekpo, Sheila Auguste, Meryl Alton, Philip Yearwood, Jerry Malcolm, Ruthven Mereigh, Nevard Malcolm, Petipha Lewis, Louisa Chase, Ope Bankole, Valery Small, Gloria Payne Banfield, Jemmie Mason-Francis, Christopher Abani, Patricia Saint-Hilaire, Chris Cudjoe Deriggs, Ludwig Laher, Dorothea Smartt, Judy Alexis, Erica Toorcen.

I am also indebted to the following for their support: Andy & Amy of the Arvon Foundation, Joan Goody, Chris Searle, Lamin Touré, Makeda Coaston, Marie Stacey, Mesfin Yohannes, Sonia McIntosh and the students of my SF460 class at Goldsmith's who question everything.

For those who came before: H.D Baptiste & Jacqueline Creft
For Binta Gaye and for those who have come after: Nichole, Janine, Akilah and Jamal.

Rum an Coke

Norma Browne got up early, cried a bit, stared at her hand and muttered to herself with a reluctant, bitter conviction, 'Was a waste. A waste!'

Nobody heard her except perhaps the boy; but even if he had, he would not remember much, come daylight.

Come daylight, he would lurch out of the house hungry, ill and angry, his body starved of something that neither she nor any food on earth could satisfy. He would be away a couple of hours or maybe the whole day and then he would return to lie below the house, the turbulence gone except in the working of his eyes. He would not be able to look at her, not until the shivering started again very late in the evening and he began, once more, to hit her.

She got up early because a thought had nudged her out of sleep, an idea - amazingly straightforward - which, with the coming daylight became a focused resolve.

She waited until he left, then dressed herself clumsily but quickly in the light blue dress that, fifteen years ago, she'd bought for his Christening and which ten years later, she also wore to take him to that special school in St. George's.

He was a beautiful boy then, clear-eyed and quick, his little body full of purpose and surprises. 'Remarkably intelligent' was what the teachers said; and to prove they were not lying, they'd written it on a pretty piece of parchment paper, framed it and handed it to her.

Not like now, she thought. Not like now at all - because what she used to feel then went way past pride. And if, in those days, she felt embarrassed or even terrified, it was only because she could hardly believe that someone like her could be so blessed.

With the same awkward haste, Norma Browne knelt and reached beneath the iron bed. She dragged out what looked like a pillow and emptied its contents on the floor. Several objects rolled out of the wads of fabric she would never use for anything but kept anyway, 'just in case': a couple of heavy silver bracelets, a ring of pure Guyana gold, an old passport with a very clear photo of a man that looked exactly like her son and a small blue book on which 'The Co-operative Bank' was printed in large letters.

She took the little book, stuffed it down her bosom and went to the main road to wait for the only bus that travelled twenty miles, twice a day, to and from St. George's.

It was evening when she returned. The migrating birds that spent the November and December months in the swamp half a mile away, were already dropping like black rain out of an inflamed sky and settling on the mangroves.

She went straight to the bedroom to replace the book and leave a small but heavy parcel beneath the bed. Then she began to look for things to do. She would have gone to the garden at the top of the hill above the village but she'd already sown more corn and peas than she had ever sown before, she'd weeded the sweet potatoes, reinforced the mud rows with wattle and bamboo, trimmed the bananas and cleared the stones which, every year, appeared miraculously in the soil. She'd put new campèche pillars under the house, added a kitchen and re-laid the yard with stones that she'd gathered from the roadside. Anything that hard work could possibly achieve to ease her days, she'd already done. And if it were possible to undo it all and start again she would gladly do so, because hard work saved her from remembering - even though she'd learnt that not remembering was not the same as forgetting. Not remembering was holding back the shame, or redirecting it the way the drains she dug during the Rainy Season turned excess water away from her garden.

She saw him coming and she got up, studying his face, his walk, the set of his mouth. It was always important that she catch his mood, because it determined how her day went, although when he returned he was never violent. He would have gone over to Teestone's house next door or to some friend of his and pumped his veins with a needleful of that milky stuff which did such dreadful things to him.

The milky stuff, she did not understand. She thought she had already seen or imagined every awful thing there was but nothing in her life had prepared her for what they called de niceness: niceness, because of the way it made them feel, they said; niceness that had sucked the life out of her child and replaced it with another sort of existence, an animated deadness that had reduced her to nothing in his eyes.

Before the deadness was the hunger. He was hungry all the time and she fed him more and more while he seemed to grow thinner by the hour. He'd also become secretive and had lost the quiet temper he was born with. When the shivering started and there was nothing she could do for him, he would scream at her and hit her.

And sometimes she wondered which was worse: his torment or her own shame before the village. Once she caught him doing it to himself panic-ridden and slobbering until he'd fed the beast inside his veins.

For this - for this especially - she did not blame him because he was her child and once, she had known him

9

differently. True, she'd seen him do a few things, some of which were a violence against her sense of decency - like the time she caught him with his cousin, younger than him by two years on her bed and she'd almost killed him - but apart from that Daniel was a perfect boy.

ooooooo

She would never know how it started, or what it was she did or did not do that made him need 'de niceness' which consumed him so completely. But now she knew who gave it to her boy and that was partly why she went to town. Nobody had told her; they'd only confirmed the truth for her.

It was that gold chain she bought him as a present that made her know. He'd asked for it before he did the exams, set himself his own condition, told her if he got an 'A' for all of them, she should buy him a gold chain with his name written on it. And of course she'd sent her macmère Grace, to St. George's to get it straight away. Then she hid it in her pillowcase and waited. And when he came home one day and told her that he'd got all his 'A's, she went straight to the bedroom and brought it out. That amazed him, not the chain but the fact that she believed he would get the 'A's just because he said so.

So when she saw that gold chain around Teestone's neck it suddenly made sense. Everything made sense: the house Teestone was improving, the way the children flocked to him, the girls warring amongst themselves for his attention.

And from then, over the months, she'd studied him. Teddy Stonewall - that boy! That boy who'd never seen a classroom in all his life, who'd never lifted a finger for his mother, who'd grown up by the roadside near the rumshop watching the world slip past; that boy who, having worked for nothing, wanted everything. And over the past months she saw the way it all came to him: the pretty clothes, the new, red Suzuki bike, other people's children. Then the large cars with darkened windows began to arrive from St. George's.

She would watch them come and go till well past midnight or till the beast awakened in Daniel's veins and she had to turn to him.

At first her interest in Teestone was incidental, no more than the curiosity of an adult in the goings-on of the young. That was in the early days when she knew nothing of the powder. She had seen Daniel suck it up his nostrils a couple of times and believed him when he told her it was no different from a sweet, a new something to tantalise the young; and she thought that it would pass like those little obsessions her boy developed from time to time and then relinquished for his books. Besides, it didn't use to make him ill and he hadn't begun to hit her.

Why she didn't think of going to see Teestone sooner amazed her. It was as if the idea had been ripening inside her and now that it had done so, she couldn't wait to meet the young man whom a powder had made so powerful, the whole world was frightened to displease him.

The rest of the day burnt itself out rapidly. Its charred remains hung indecisively over the houses of the village. Her boy had begun to stir in sleep.

With a series of rapid, nervous movements she straightened her dress, left her house and crossed over to Teestone's yard.

He came out when she called, his body blocking the doorway completely. She had to look up to examine his face against the darkness of the door-mouth. This she did quickly before bringing her head back down. Now she watched him with her eyes upturned.

'What you want, Miss Lady.'

'I want to come in,' she said.

'Come in where!' He glared down at her. 'Come inside o my house! What you want in my house?'

'Is someting,' she lowered her voice and her eyes, afraid that he would not let her in. 'Is someting I want to buy. I kin pay,' she added hastily.

'I tell you I sellin anyting? What you waan to buy!' He was still fuming but his voice, like hers, was lowered.

'I waan some niceness,' she said flatly and lifted her eyes at him. He paused a moment, shifted his body and she slipped under his arm. Teestone pulled the door behind him.

Now that the door was closed, he was suddenly transformed, almost like another person. Relaxed, smiling, he drew a wooden stool from under the mahogany table in the middle of the room and placed it before her. Carefully, Norma Browne lowered herself.

Teestone grinned at her unease. 'Miss Norma what you say you want?'

'I jus waan some, some of dat ting dat make my son, make my son so happy.' She halted on the last word, made it sound like the most frightful thing on earth. But she managed a smile and that put Teestone at ease. He seated himself a few feet in front of her. He smiled wider and she noticed the gold tooth. She did not remember him having a gold tooth. He had bad teeth anyway, the sort that prised his lips apart permanently.

The shirt she also noticed, was of a soft material that dropped as if it were liquid; made, no doubt, from one of those fabulous materials she had seen in pictures in Grace's magazines, and in the large stores through whose wide glass windows you feasted your eyes but never entered because the light-skinned woman at the counter and the way everything was laid out just told you that you! you'd better not come in.

'What you offerin?' he whispered, and for a moment she did not understand him. 'What you have?' he repeated.

She allowed her eyes to wander around the room before easing her fingers down her bosom and pulling out an old handkerchief. It was rolled into a knot. The thin hands held it curiously, the curl of the fingers accentuating their frailty. There was a scar at the back of her left hand, as if she had been burnt there, very badly, once. The fingers un-knotted the bit of cloth to reveal a ball of crumpled notes.

'A thousand dollars,' she said and dropped it on the table. It was all she had. The gesture said so, that and her trembling hands. She was never likely to have that much again, for it had taken a lot from her to get it. One thousand dollars that would have gone to her boy along with the house and the piece of land that had been in the family for as long as anyone could remember.

Teestone did not reach for the money, in fact he looked at her as if he were seeing her for the first time; a sudden probing interest, and something like suspicion because she was offering all of it to him. But she was an old woman, in trouble and confused because her son was in trouble and confused. Because now, her son belonged to him, his eyes barely concealed his hostility. The stupid kind. The kind he despised most: those women who would do anything to please their sons, who never saw the sky because, all their lives, they were too busy looking down, digging and scratching the earth; demeaning and denying themselves for what? It always puzzled him how people like that ever came by money. A thousand dollars! And it was already his. All of it. It had always been his! For if she had not given it to him herself, her son would have, eventually, bit by bit. They were all coming now, these old women. When their children could no longer get to him on their own, they were the ones who came and begged for them. Norma Browne was not the first, and she would not be the last. And the best part was, these days he did not have to do a thing. These days money, wherever it was, made its way to him.

'Hold on,' he told her, opening the door behind him and disappearing into his bedroom.

Slowly, her eyes travelled around the room.

In the centre of a tiny table in the corner there was a framed picture of Teestone, his mother, and the man his mother had lived with but who, she knew without a doubt, wasn't his father at all, although she'd made the man believe he was. To the right of that there was another photo of a child.

Having nothing better to do, Norma Browne examined the picture of the baby sitting on a straw mat staring out at the camera with a child's wide-eyed, open-mouthed, bewilderment. He hadn't grown out of that wide, wet mouth, nor indeed those eyes that seemed smaller than they really were because of the heaviness of the lids. She replaced the picture, cautiously.

He was rebuilding the house his mother had left him, or rather he was replacing the wood with concrete, which meant erecting blocks against the board walls outside. When they were set in cement he would knock the planks out one by one from inside. Now, even before he'd done that, the wet concrete was seeping through the boards, leaving a pale sediment which, when she passed her hand along it, left an ugly trace of powder and tiny bits of wood on her fingers. Electrical wires ran everywhere: along the floorboards, the ceiling and the walls, and she realised that the rumours she'd heard were true. Teestone was bringing electricity to his house. Or he was having that man who came in the long, black car on Fridays - that man they called The Blade - make the government do it for him. A couple of large, soft chairs lay upturned in a corner, completely covered with transparent plastic, and to the left of her there was a gaping hole through which she could see the earth below the house. Perhaps they had opened it up, she speculated, because he was replacing the wooden pillars too.

The smell of concrete was everywhere: intrusive, corrosive - as brash as the youths who, wherever she turned, were remaking everything, upsetting everything, undoing everything - the way wood mites secretly hollowed out a house and all the while you did not know that you were surrounded by nothing until a small wind passed one day and blew it down around you.

She was still contemplating this scene of quiet devastation when Teestone came out with a small brown bag, the type the shop sold sugar by the half pound in. He did not place it in her hand but on the mahogany table in front of them. She took it up with a confident gesture and for a moment, in fact for the first time, she seemed different, self-possessed.

She opened the bag carefully and clumsily dragged out the small plastic sac that was folded inside it.

'S'not a lot,' she said, shocked. 'Not a lot for all my money.'

Teestone laughed then, laughed till the fat vein at the side of his neck stood out. Fascinated, she watched that neck-vein throb and pulse with laughter. 'S'what you expect? Dis, dis worth more dan it weight in gold, y'know dat? More-dan-it-weight-in-gold.' He spoke the last few words as if they were one, as though he'd rehearsed it till it sounded that way: rhythmic and convincing. 'Ask anybody.' Teestone added, emphatically.

'Didn know,' she apologised and then she brought it to her nose. She froze, fixing very dark eyes on him. 'It s'pose to smell like dat? Like, uh, baby powder?' She was looking at him closely but he did not notice this. What he saw was a small woman, old before her time, almost doubled over with hard work, with a nervous hand and a frightened voice, trying to get some stuff off him. His contempt had denied him any of the details. And so he had no sense of her: the very, very steady eyes, the tight-set mouth that had lost or given up the habit of laughter, a generous forehead partly covered by an old head wrap and a tendency to follow his every movement.

Her question took him completely by surprise. The slight narrowing of his eyes and the way he tried to close his mouth without really managing it, confirmed her suspicion.

'It not s'pose to smell o baby powder,' she told him quietly, a new hardness in her voice.

15

Is so it smell, he was about to tell her, and ask her what de hell she know 'bout niceness anyway, but her directness stopped him, that and her very steady gaze. He snatched the packet off the table and went back inside the bedroom. This time he returned sooner, dropped a different packet on the table and sat back heavily.

Norma took it up and passed it under her nose. She could see by his expression that he wanted her to leave. He was tired, or perhaps, now that his business with her was over, he wanted to get rid of her. But she was not finished with him yet.

She wanted to know how she should prepare the stuff and he showed her. Her hands shook when she took the needle to examine the thin, evil thread of metal that slipped so easily into flesh. The first time she saw her boy use it, it had made her sick. He had taken it standing and had fallen straight back against the floorboards, his body rigid, like a tree deprived suddenly of its roots, doing nothing to break the fall. He'd cut his head badly and did not even know it, just laid there with that smile, that awful inner peace, while she turned him over and tended to his wound.

In her hand the metal shone like an amber thread of light against the lamp.

'All of it is for de boy?' asked Teestone, showing her his tooth.

Some was for her son, she answered, and well, she was goin to use de rest. Was de niceness nicer if she used all of it in one go?

No, he told her, and the gold tooth glimmered in the light. If she used more than he just showed her - at that he pulled out a pack of razor blades, extracted one, opened the packet he'd handed her and separated a small portion, working it with the same care that she used to mix medicine for her boy's illness when he was a child. If she ever used more than that, he pointed at the tiny heap he'd separated, it would kill her.

'Too much niceness does kill. Y'unnerstan?' He laughed at his own joke, lit a cigarette and leaned back against the chair. That too was new, the long cigarettes with the bit of silver at the end; in fact everything about Teestone was new, even his face. There was not the redness in the eyes, the dreadful tiredness that went deeper than age, the loosening of something precious and essential in the face, the damp surrender of the skin - once smooth and dark and beautiful with youth - to that terrible hunger that made her son strike out at her. Teestone looked fresh and happy and as alert as a cat. Money had made him handsome.

Suddenly she felt relaxed. 'Could ha been a nice house,' she said, looking around the room, smiling the smallest of smiles, happier now than she had been for the past twelve months, from the time she discovered that her son was stuffing his veins with poison.

It was perhaps out of that odd sense of abeyance that she reached out suddenly and fixed Teestone's collar; or, she might have been prodded by a desire to get an idea of what that shiny material really felt like. Her fingers brushed the side of his neck, touching the laughing vein which made him recoil with a violence she thought entirely undue.

She pretended not to notice his outrage, got up slowly and shuffled towards the door. There, she stopped and turned back to Teestone.

'He lef school last year,' she told him with a quiet, neutral look. 'My Dan jus come an tell me dat he leavin school, and I say, 'You can't. You can't because you always tell me dat you want to see de world, dat you'll make me proud and build a nicer house for us when you become someting. You say you see how hard it is for me. How much I does do for you and how much I'll always do for you.' An he laugh, like he was laughing at someting he know inside he head. He say he don't need to go nowhere no more to see de world, because he could see it from right dere where he lie down whole day on

17

he back below my house. He tell me what he see sometimes and I can't make no sense of it. Cos I can't see inside mih little boy head. I can't make no sense o people walkin over precipice an dem not dyin, o animal dat talk an laugh with you inside you head. I can't. But he say he see dem and it make im happy.

But is when de niceness get bad,' she added softly, apologetically, 'and I can't do nothing and I just hear im bawl an bawl an bawl, an he start hittin me, dat I does - well I does jus tek it.

Y'know sometimes he hit me - my son? Hit me like he father used to?' Her voice had dropped to a whisper and it was thick and dark and gentle, and tinged with a terrible sadness. 'I let im. I let im till he get tired an fall asleep. He don sleep no more like he used ter. Is like someting in he sleep, in he dreamin beatin im up same like he do wid me. All de time. Dat's why - dat's why I does...'

Teestone got up suddenly. 'You get what you want, Miss Lady. Go!'

He'd already pushed open the door for her.

Norma Browne walked out into a close, choked night that had settled on the village like a blanket, and beyond which nothing - not even the screaming of those birds in the swamp - seemed to escape.

There were some girls outside, a few of them not more than fourteen years old, their precocious eyes fixing her incredulously, and then an instant later turning to the doorway with that still and hungry gaze she'd seen so often in her son during the quiet times when the shivering stopped and she'd force- fed him or tried to. She knew all of them. Some she'd even delivered before her hand went funny. Or, as children, she'd kept them for their mothers when they went off to St. George's for medicine or some necessary thing that their hillside gardens or the sea could not provide.

At their age, she thought, life was supposed to be kinder - as it had been, even for her; an enormous promise which never lasted long, but was part of growing up. It belonged to that age. Was part of what kept you going for the rest of your life. And you should not miss it.

She decided not to go home. Her boy would be there now beneath the house laid out on his back sleeping or talking to himself. He would remain there until she came and brought him in. Or if she did not feel like it, she would leave him there until he was conscious again - perhaps some time close to morning - when he would beat her door until she let him in. Tonight he would not touch her because she had what it took to quiet him.

And that was another thing: he would not beg anymore, not offer Teestone anything - anything at all for the relief of a needle. Once she saw him beg and it had shamed her. Saw him do it yesterday and it had shamed her even more because Teestone's refusal had brought him raging to her yard.

She took the track that ran off from the main road, which used to take him to the school he'd won the scholarship for in St. George's.

It was a long, hard walk because the rains from the weeks before had made a drain of the mud track. The pebbles slipped under her feet and she was forced to steady her progress by grabbing at the bushes on the side. Ordinarily, she would have taken a bottle torch but that was only when she planned a visit; tonight, the parcel held firmly in her hand, it had suddenly seemed like common sense that she should visit Grace. It was Grace who first told her about Daniel: how on mornings when he left for school he got off the bus a mile away, and doubled back to feed his veins all day on Teestone's powder. It was Grace who, without moving from her house, had found out where it came from and the nickname of the government man that visited Teestone every Friday night.

Grace was the only one to whom she spoke these days. Grace, with the cat's eyes, who used to have the gentlest of husbands; whose five daughters had all gone away and sent her money every month, from England, America and Canada; who'd offered to buy her son's uniform as a little present for winning the scholarship. Grace who always got much more than she deserved from life.

The back of her hand was itching; a deep, insistent itch that she could not reach because it was beneath the skin. Years ago, her left hand did not scratch that way, nor was there the white scar at the back of it where the skin had been cut away and then healed very badly. And it did not curl itself up as it did now. Many people, those who did not remember or rather those that forgot too easily, thought she had been born that way but Grace remembered that she wasn't. Grace remembered everything.

Grace's place was neat and small and full of colour. There were large blood-red hibiscus on her curtains and the enamelled bowls and cups, and the glasses in the cabinet had bouquets of flowers patterned all over them. Even her dress was a flower garden. God had given her eyes that shone like bits of coloured glass which, depending on her mood, were exactly like a cat's. Her friend burned three kerosene lamps instead of one. Big lamps - the ones marked 'Home Sweet Home' in white on the shade - that they sold for ten dollars at Everybody's store in St. George's. Their combined brightness gave an amazing, shadowless quality to the room.

Grace settled her down and retreated to the kitchen. She returned with a bowl of soup and handed it to Norma who looked hesitantly up at her.

'Eat!' she grunted.

'I done eat arready.'

'Den eat again. When trouble eatin people, people have to eat back! So take de food an eat!'

The sweet smell of stewed peas and provision and salt meat almost made her faint. She hadn't eaten and Grace knew that she was lying. These days, she'd lost her appetite for everything. Most times she forgot to eat at all.

She placed the packet on the table and took up the bowl. Grace looked at the brown bag frankly, a question in her eyes.

'How's de boy?' she mumbled, still staring at the paper bag.

'Cost me everything. All dat was left; a thousand dollars,' Norma said it as if the 'everything' was more important than the money.

'What cost what?' asked Grace.

'Dat.' Norma nudged the bag with the handle of the spoon.

Grace reached for it and opened it. The powder was on her fingers when she withdrew her hand. It could have been the effect of the candlelight on her silver bracelets but her hand seemed to tremble. The woman's face went dead. 'A thousand dollars! Fo-'

'Dat,' Norma Browne said, herself quietly appalled. 'De rest of de money. What left. I draw it out today.'

'Jeezas Christ, you, you buy dat poison for you boy! You mad!'

Norma Browne continued eating, but she looked up and exposed her face to Grace.

'You think so?' She muttered with complete unconcern. And that left a chill in Grace's stomach.

'Where he is?' Grace asked.

'Below de house. Sleepin.' Norma swallowed. 'He tired.'

'Still - erm - hittin you?' Grace went completely still.

Norma stopped short, the bit of meat held contemplatively between her thumb and index finger. She nodded.

'First de father and den de son. God bless me I don have no boy chile. But I wish, I wish I had a boy to raise he hand and touch me! Jeezan bread, I wish dat if..' she stopped breathless, eyes flaming in the lamplight. 'God forgive me but I'll make dat sonuvabitch wish he never born.'

Norma smiled, 'Dat's de problem. You don see? If he's a son ova bitch, dat mean I is de bitch dat make dis son. I don wish he never born but sometimes, sometimes I wish he don live no more. To ease, to ease im up a bit.' She looked up apologetically.

Grace grunted irritably. 'You - you not goin to let im continue!'

'Nuh.' Norma licked her fingers. 'Nuh, I goin stop im. Tonight.'

The certitude in her voice made Grace lean closer. 'You goin ter... Jeezas, girl. Jeezas!'

'I not goin ter, y'know. But like I say, I think of it sometimes - sometimes, all de time - for a whole day, I think of it. If y'all hear im bawlin, not to bother. Tell everybody not to bother.' Something in her tone turned Grace's eyes to Norma's hand, the one that lay curled up like a bird's claw in her lap.

That hand alone was reason enough for everyone to bother. What kind of woman would place her hand between the cogs of a machine so that she could get the insurance to send her boy off to a high-class school in St. George's. Inside a canemill besides! And if she could do that to herself for him, what on God's earth wouldn't she do to make her sacrifice worthwhile?

'Go easy,' muttered Grace, taking up the bowl of unfinished food and heading for the kitchen. It was both a warning and a farewell and sensing this, Norma got up.

'If you hear him,' she started.

'Uh-huh,' Grace answered - a little too brusquely perhaps, without turning round. 'Rum-an-coke is what dey call it,' she called out from the kitchen. 'Dey take dat ting and drink down rum right after. Dat's what make dem mad an beat up deir own flesh-an-blood so bad.'

'Ah know.' Norma curled her hand around the packet. All of a sudden the room felt too bright for her. She lifted her bad hand above her eyes as if to shade them from the sun. She paused briefly at the doorway, made as if to say something then changed her mind before slipping out into the night.

Back home, she helped the boy from under the house and led him to the bedroom. He was quiet and aware of her but she knew that soon he would be shivering. She lit the lamp, undressed him and bathed him like she used to. The way she thought she'd forgotten. And then she went back to the kitchen.

There, she carved out a portion of the stuff exactly as she'd seen Teestone do. She knew where he kept his needle, knew what she had to do.

She went in. Laid the small bag down beside the door. He'd already begun to shiver.

'C'mon Bumpsy, take this for mammy,' she said, speaking to him exactly as she would to a baby; and he seemed, from somewhere deep inside, to recognise that tone; began curling his shirt ends between his fingers like he used to when he was a child, while he looked at her with a tired, helpless uncertainty.

'Is for you. Tek it from Mammy,' she urged, the voice soft and angry at the same time.

He took the needle and she watched him unflinching, while he served himself, so hungry for the ease it offered he was almost sobbing. And then while he recovered and then began floating away from her, she reached below the bed, opened the bag and took out the length of chain and the padlocks she had bought in St. George's. Still cooing her mummy-talk, Norma Browne fastened her son against the bed.

If you hear im bawlin, she'd told Grace - who would, come morning, pass the message on to everyone - If you hear im bawlin, tell everybody not to bother. And she knew the bawling would begin soon, or some time in the morning, or perhaps the next day, and it would go on for a long, long time.

Back in the kitchen she mixed most of what remained of the powder in the paper bag. Finished, she leaned out of her window and observed the precocious girls, the motorbikes, the occupants of the occasional car sneaking back and forth between the road and Teestone's house.

Soon the traffic would subside, the lamps go out and the whole world come to a pause while Teestone slept.

It is a warm, tense night - lonely too because there is nobody to talk to and the sound of the wind, and the great, starless emptiness above her makes her think of futile distances, of the irreconcilable vastness of the world, her own smallness, and the place she feels she no longer has in it. Because a time does reach, she thinks, when a woman can only hope for what come after she: she children and de children dat will come from dem, that would pass on and on and on, if not her name, then her blood and perhaps a memory of her; an acknowledgment that they were alive only because she existed once. Dat, dat's what does mek life worth someting.

Her hand is itching again and she thinks that perhaps it will rain. Her hand always iches before it rains. She is slightly anxious. A low wind stirs the air, shakes the trees above the houses and leaves a smell of cinnamon, swamp and charcoal over the village. As if this were a signal, she straightens up, steps out into the night. Full height, she is much taller than most people have seen her, and she has lost her shuffle as she walks across the yard. She is as soundless as the shadows that move throughout the early night to and from Teestone's house, and just as silent when she climbs his steps.

She remembers the hole in the living room and avoids it. She carries a very clear picture in her head of the house and everything in it.

The lamp is lit in his bedroom and he is asleep, rolled over on one side and snoring softly. He is naked. One of the girls lies curled up in front of him, naked also, the young hips turned inwards, giving her a curious air of innocence. Sleep has also stripped away what remains of the womanishness she wears by day, almost like another garment, and has made of her a girl again.

She kneels beside Teestone and he stirs, perhaps sensing her in sleep.

The jab wakes him. He erupts out of sleep, his hand clutching that laughing vein at the side of his neck, but she is strong and she keeps him and the needle there until she empties it of her thousand dollars worth of niceness. Eyes wide, Teestone stares at her. His fist closes on her wrist. It is the bad hand that he is crushing and it hurts. But she smiles that dark, beautiful and alluring smile; something wonderful to take with him, she seems to say.

He eases back on the pillow releasing her and sighing the longest, most restful of all sighs, his face still incredulous, still profoundly outraged.

The girl has not stirred from sleep, and for that Norma Browne is grateful.

She walks out of the house, turns and spits carelessly at the dark before crossing to her yard.

Before she goes in, she pauses, turns her face up at the sky and sniffs. She could smell the morning. But it is still dark. And the world and the birds down there are very, very quiet.

A Different Ocean

Day yawns and cracks the egg of dawn (Stridal)

By that time she had long become familiar with the play of light on the tiny whisky bottles frosted by the waves, the fantastical chunks of multi-coloured glass, reshaped by salt and time. She'd scrubbed the coins and strips of green-caked copper until they became once more as bright as the fire that had shaped them.

What astonished her nephew, Cedric and her friends was the fact that the sea had delivered these things, which they themselves had never been able to locate. It was as if it required a particular way of seeing, a talent that was specific to the Sienna Millers of this world.

And indeed Sienna saw the bay below their homes in a very different way from them. It was the great wide open paw of some soft-voiced, growling dog that scampered off to other worlds at night to fetch these gifts for her. So, on mornings, when she sneaked down to the beach she found them waiting there amongst the shells, the jellyfish and seaweeds.

The doll had been her greatest find. She had simply found it on the beach one morning, a pale, outlandish flower sprawled against the glittering blackness of the sand. It possessed half of everything: a single, sea-bleached leg that was cocked up at the sky in a most indecorous manner, one damaged eye that seemed to follow her movements whichever way she turned and a portion of an arm. It had half a headful of soft, corn-yellow hair, which made her recognise its possibilities straight away.

She'd bathed it and dressed it. Had cared for it the way a person would care for an ailing friend, having forced on herself a secret and very pleasant conviction that it would fulfil the miracle that its very discovery on the sand had promised: to restore itself completely and become whole again.

Not only had she named the doll Lucille, they'd quickly become sisters. And by virtue of that carefully worked out fact of kinship, she too had acquired sun-coloured hair that floated around her face, not unlike Lucille's, hair which she squinted through, combed and parted with her fingers and shook constantly in pleasantly annoying, imaginary winds. She and Lucille, they now lived in a blue room with pretty yellow curtains and windows that faced a flush of trees, laden with apples and pears and peaches, all growing on the same branch. The tar had also seeped away from beneath her skin, leaving her as pink as the cheek of the one-eyed doll. And to cap the whole thing off she had changed her name to Jane.

Tan Lin threw Lucille into the fire the evening Sienna, in a fit of excitement, forgot her in the yard and hastened down to the beach to watch the men haul in a giant octopus from the place they called The Mouth.

She bawled and railed like an orphan while Cedric, his face a mix of sympathy and pleasure, poked the black, sizzling lump of foul-smelling plastic from the fire and placed it at her feet.

'Chiiiile! Shut dat big black mout o yours before I close it for you for good,' Tan Lin shouted. And Sienna didn't wait for the words that were sure to follow. Words that were worse

27

than all the cursings she could think of. Words whose meaning she did not know exactly but which nevertheless, would ride the air and sting her like a splattering of hot oil. She was halfway down the hill and heading for the beach when those words she hated so much came, '*Petit jamette laid!*'

They propelled her forward as surely as if somebody had planted an oversized boot on her behind. And it was only when her feet hit the soft and somehow allaying coolness of the sand and she saw the small crowd at the northern end of the bay that she stopped the bawling, her rancour not so much replaced as distracted by the sight of the small crowd, for they were standing on the part of the beach they habitually warned strangers against.

The sign that used to read DANGER, SUDDEN DROP, in big red letters was still there although the writing had long been chewed into by rust. And the sea as if in complicity with the faded sign, did its best to hide the crater the government had dug there on a promise to build a yacht marina in The Silent. But at the end of that election year, the machines they'd sent to excavate the shallows had climbed back onto the trucks and never did return. What they left there was a patch of darker blue which only reminded them of itself in odd ways: a sudden flush of cold along the stomach of the person who dared to swim across it, or the way a boat or bit of wood would slowly drift towards it, in response to some secret pull, some quiet, dreadful persuasion which, they reminded themselves time and time again, had already swallowed the lives of two unsuspecting brothers. And it was this unearthly readiness to suck in everything that possessed a will weaker than its own that made them call that place The Mouth.

Sienna decided that they might have spotted another octopus down there, for it was a place these ocean creatures liked. Several strides away, she realised that it was Missa Jacko who was in the middle of the group talking, his oar-thin arms like propeller blades flailing the morning air above the heads of men and women. Soon, his words like a flap of agitated gulls reached her.

'Some thief-an-criminal gone off and take mih fishpot and all the fish that was in it. I goin to murder the dog. I goin to search every house-an-garden. I goin to inspect every latrine in the area. I goin to scrutinise every fishpot in the sea and no matter how much paint dem paint to change it, is goin I goin to find mih property. Is only a stinkin thief could thief de fishpot dat I buy de other day. It was full of fish, I sure o dat, else why de hell dey thief it? Eh? I want back all mih fish in mih fishpot. Who de hell dey tink dem is, eh? Who dem tink I is!'

If the others were alarmed, it was not so much at the fact that somebody had stolen Jacko's fishpot but that his awful complaining voice would rub against their ears like an unrelenting corn husk for at least another month - including nights - since Jacko was the kind of man who did not need an audience to run a conversation. Even those who had no memory could not forget the time when Martin bought him a pound of hooks in town and forgot to give him back his penny change.

Sienna's arrival turned the man's rum-reddened eyes on her. His hands froze on something in mid air, her presence presenting him with a possibility he hadn't thought about before.

'You! You know anyting about my fishpot?'

The astonishment stopped her midstride. Catching her breath and swallowing a sudden sting of tears she bawled, 'Me? Me! Me tief yuh fishpot? Me! Me?- I goin tell my Tanty dat you say ...'

Jacko's hands fluttered in alarm. 'Tell yuh Tanty! Tell yuh Tanty...is only ask I ask, an I ask polite. I didn say...'

'I goin tell she, I goin tell she dat you say everybody in we family is thief an you goin search from de top o we house to below we bed an even we latrine an...'.

'Jeezas - spare me,' Jacko turned to the faces around him, his lips shaping an appeal. 'Anybody here hear me say anyting like dat? As God is me witness, anybody hear dem wuds come from me?'

'Wasn't what you say', Anna May cut in sourly. 'But who is to say is not what you mean? What mek you tink is not dat foreign boat down dere dat cut you fishpot.'

Ten pairs of eyes turned towards 'down there'.

'Down there' was The Silent - a largish lagoon of still dark water that sat directly below the precipice on which their houses stood. It was a place that yachts liked. They started arriving in November like a flock of great white birds. So tall sometimes their sail-wings seemed to scrape the blue above. They would remain there for a couple of days or sometimes for a week.

A beautiful skiff with a very long mast was sitting in the middle of The Silent. It hadn't been there the day before. It must have arrived late last night or in the small hours of that morning.

The man's hand milled unbelievingly above their heads but before he could draw breath Anna May's voice slapped him around the ear. 'So! What you goin tell me now - dat whiteman boat never does cut no fishpot rope?'

Everything happened quickly then. Martin pulled his diving glass over his face and rushed the water. And of course he headed for The Mouth. He began hovering around the edges like an insect at the lip of some godforsaken flower. Then his voice rang out across the water with more pleasure than surprise. 'It down there! Kin hardly see it! Look like it full o fish too.' His laughter had the sharpness and abruptness of a gull's. It tickled the small crowd into a sudden derisive burst and Jacko's shoulders became a defeated slump.

Before they realised it, Sienna had hit the water in a rapid running dive. The momentum carried her right through to the blue lip of The Mouth. She caught Martin unawares, saw the rush of alarm the instant she surfaced beside him. She sucked in hard and arced her body in a tight, downward curve, flashing her heels briefly, defiantly in his face.

The cold swallowed her whole and bruised her senses. She swam fast downwards towards the dim unearthly shapes below, already aware of the growing pressure in her chest and eardrums even as she puzzled at the ease with which she was slipping down the throat of the hole. Her body was telling her something that her mind already knew: water should resist. The sea never offered itself up to anyone that easily.

But she kept kicking, heading for the bottom-darkness until she spotted the white blur that was the rope that had secured the float to the fishpot. The wicker of the pot itself was no more than a patch of paleness somewhere further down. She focused on the rope, kicking harder as she reached for it, amazed at the way it evaded her grasp. It was then she noticed the circling dance it made, understood what that meant and told herself that there shouldn't be no tide here trying to drag her down below. She milled her legs furiously, reached out and finally grasped the dancing rope. She wrapped it around her wrist and ignoring the burning in her chest, began the struggle upwards. Her efforts to fight the water's tug and haul the weight up at the same time forced her towards the other side and there suddenly, miraculously the water opened up its fist and released her.

Hands were waiting to lift her out and seat her at the back of Ragman's little boat. Jacko was bawling like a strangling goat and there was a dizzying din of voices on the beach.

They rowed her over quickly and dropped her on the sand, examining her as they would some creature that the ocean had unexpectedly deposited at their feet. The morning had become a bright, featureless haze and she could not control the trembling.

'Cold down dere,' she chattered, gathering her clothes. 'Real cold.'

'One hundred and ninety,' Martin said, his voice soft and disbelieving. 'I count one hundred and ninety.'

A quietness had descended on them all. Anna May sketched the sign of the cross across her chest and muttered something while the rest stared at the fishpot at Jacko's feet.

'You could ha dead,' Jacko muttered coarsely, and then after a pause, 'But nobody can't say is I who send you.' He seemed to be addressing the thrashing mass of parrotfish and snappers.

'Dat's all y'have to say?' His words roused something cold and bitter in Sienna.

'Yuh didn drown.' Jacko shrugged.

'De fish is mine,' she told him.

'Like hell.'

Anna May laughed softly. It alerted Jacko like a dog confronting danger, for that chuckle carried a threat that suddenly roused her son. Big and wordless as a boulder, Preeso stepped between the fishpot and the man.

'Not, not even a little one for me?'

'Not even.' Sienna told him.

Anna May did not accept the fish Sienna offered her. She seemed somehow more concerned to get off the beach, as if she'd just sensed a change in the weather. Even Jacko, now that he had recovered his possession had lost interest in it. Their sudden detachment had reduced her effort to nothing and she remained there feeling the way those awful words from Tan Lin made her feel.

That was how the two strangers met her; alone on the beach with a pile of dead fish at her feet, staring blankly at the dark blue patch of water that had left a freezing place inside of her.

She had not heard them approaching and that still puzzled her. The first time she knew they were standing there beside her was when a soft voice brushed against her ear. 'Nice catch.'

She looked round to see a woman in a sky-blue bikini smiling down on her. And for no reason she could put a finger on, her heart began to race. Perhaps it was because the woman was slim as the dolls Sienna had seen in the St. George's store the first and only Christmas Eve she'd ever been to town. Dolls with skin as pale and pure as manioc starch. The woman had their pink cheeks and Lucille's creamy yellow hair. And her eyes - her eyes especially - the girl stared at them dumbfounded for it was as if they had been made especially for her from a patch of perfect sky. And even more astonishing was the fact that they matched exactly the little stone set in silver, fixed to a very fine chain around her neck.

'I'm Sue - Sue Kramer. This is John Hedgcoe.'

'Hi,' the man said. His eyes were very different from Sookramer's, a dark centre rimmed by a lighter colour, which she could not determine exactly. The eyes of birds, she thought, seagulls. He was barefooted like the woman, a bit taller, and like Miss Sookramer, everything about him was gold, even the hairs covering his stomach and limbs.

Nothing in her life had prepared her for this encounter. For these strangers who came in from the other side of the world never seemed to see them in their little houses on the hill. And she understood this. For wasn't their world like the pretty glass boxes that Cedric had shown her in that magazine, in which people placed and cultivated fish that looked like flowers? Their yachts came and went with the same seasonal indifference of seabirds and if it were true that they exchanged the occasional stand-offish smile from time to time, it was only during some chance early-morning or late-night encounter on the beach which were never planned or natural. If these people belonged to the same world at all, they certainly owned very different parts of it.

So when the woman held out her hand Sienna could not help but stare at it and then up at her face. She could not hold those eyes so she fixed instead the blue of the stone.

What was her name? The woman's voice was soft and pleasantly musical. Sienna Miller? That was a nice name. Did they all have English names? In which of those houses on the hill did she live? Why did they build their homes on stilts? Did she know the names of the fish at her feet? Where did she learn to dive like that? A whole raft of questions the answers to which generated even more questions.

The man who had never taken his eyes off her spoke only when the woman paused for breath. And his was an odd way of speaking since she could not decide whether he was talking to the woman, himself or her. 'Nice teeth', he said. That was when she was in the middle of responding to one of the woman's questions. And in between another of her replies, 'good shoulders, deep ribs' and something else which wasn't clear at all.

Miss Sookramer excused herself and stooped to prise a shell from the sand. The man spoke to Sienna directly for the first time. Did she know why The Mouth behaved the way it did? Did she know that the whole ocean was like that, more or less?

'Warmer water rises to the top, colder water slides below; the way water boils'.

For some reason, he added with a quiver of the little gold moustache, the effect was much stronger in The Mouth. Were there others, boys, who could dive like her?

'I is de best.' She answered flatly which made the man laugh softly. And pleased that she had humoured him, Sienna added for emphasis, 'everybody round here know dat.'

The man smiled brightly down at her before pointing at a small white craft in the lagoon. It was a blinding silver in the path of the morning sun. 'That one *Cincinnati Dreams* is ours.' He grinned at the morning and the sea. 'Ever been on one before?'

Sienna shook her head.

'Wanna come over later? Susan thinks you're nice.'

'Tell us what time, we'll come in the dinghy and get you.' The woman offered.

'I kin swim,' the girl said flashing a quick instinctive glance up at the houses.

The man was looking out to sea, his eyes so narrowed down, all she saw there was a glint. She might have told him that it was Missa Mosan's little tray of a boat, coming in from his trip out to the reefs beyond Goat Point. In fact she hadn't remembered Missa Mosan when they asked her if anyone could dive better than she did. But, she decided, he should not be counted anyway since everybody knew he'd exchanged his wife and children's soul to the devil for the secrets of the deep. And he was not from The Silent anyway. He came from that barren place, several hills beyond that was known curiously as The Waterhole. She also knew that he'd borrowed the eyes of gulls, which was why he saw things from great distances before anyone else had an idea they were there.

'Well, we'd better be off,' the man said briskly.

'See yah later,' Sookramer said, and she was also off, hurrying to keep up with the man.

They left behind a slight wind, full of odours, which came off the sea and wrapped itself around her like a piece of cloth. She sniffed and grinned. She'd taught herself to pry beneath the first fresh layer of any seawind to get at the smells it always carried underneath - those magical and secret odours that arrived from the very place she believed Lucille had come from.

'Look like you conversatin wit de sea!' Missa Mosan was a little man with a big head and the largest hands she'd ever seen. He was smiling as if he expected her to be waiting there for him.

'Is true you have a thousan chilren?' she asked him promptly. She'd asked this question hundreds of times before, but she knew that if he chose to answer her at all, it would be as if he'd heard it for the first time.

'How much twelve you got in a thousan, Miss?'

'A whole heap,' she muttered frowning. 'Is true you use to have a hundred girlfriend?' This one was supposed to catch him unawares but the man grinned toothlessly and winked. 'What you fink?'

She shrugged, wondering how he would react if she also told him that Tan Lin said she didn know what women saw in the big-head little runt of a man.

He began tossing things from the boat onto the sand, first his machete, then the oars, followed by his fish-gun, then a crocus bag still writhing with his catch.

'Dem pretty?'

'Dem...?'

'Yuh chilren? Dem pretty?'

He rested very large and heavy eyes on her face. 'You know anybody who not?'

'No,' she answered quickly.

'Which make me ask meself what people who does never have one word to crack with we, what dem want with one of us, specially a little girl?'

She stared at him tight-lipped but he did not seem to be in a hurry for an answer. He stepped back and reached beneath the stern of the craft, his hands emerging with something large and heavy. Whatever it was, he'd wrapped it in a piece of sacking and she watched his face as he reached into the bag, brought it out and turned it towards her. It was a shell - one of the largest she had ever seen - caked outside with silt and seaweed. But its mouth, now that it was turned to her, snatched her breath away. She had seen a queen shell only once before and it had never been this close up; and even then she had never imagined that a thing on earth could be so beautiful. For the ocean had gathered all the colours in the world, mixed them with the light of all the sunsets there had ever been and trapped them within the hollows of that shell.

'Now dat's pretty,' he breathed. 'Dese belong to de ocean. Her pussnal joolry an she never give dem up without a fight. Every time mih ooman have a chile, she send me off to get one so I kin risk mih life like she. You gotta go down, down, down an keep goin till you don't know top from bottom. You keep goin cos iffen you tink o de hurtin in yuh ears, iffen you tink one little second dat you can't reach it, den you never goin to get it. You ever wonder why all de good tings in life so flippin hard to get?'

She nodded because she had actually wondered.

He turned the shell to face him, awed it seemed, at the beauty of the thing and the fear it held for him each time he tried to draw even with his woman. And then he handed it to her. Mosan was looking at her closely when she brought the shell to her ear. She closed her eyes to absorb its thunder, the suck and surge that were also bellow and sigh, to feel the quiet unnameable stir of fear and pleasure in her gut.

Sienna opened her eyes and nodded. What he saw on her face must have satisfied him because he showed her all his gums. 'Like I say, nice tings don't come easy.'

He gathered his things and placed them in his big canvas bag. With a toss of his head, he muttered, 'watch yerself, girl! Some people don smile to smile; some-a-dem smile to bite.'

She took in those last words the way she took in Tan Lin's curses, a sort of condemnation which, even if they were directed at the strangers, felt like they were meant for her.

Still, during what remained of the day Missa Mosan's words had come to her off and on with the annoying persistence of a fly.

They did not prevent her from swimming over to the boat that evening as she'd promised. The uneasiness had washed itself off the moment she slipped into the water even if it was the first time she had ever swum in the lagoon.

Sookramer and the man welcomed her. They had drawn the boat closer to the mangroves so that if people were looking down from the houses on the hill they would not see her being lifted aboard by her new friends. There was something nice about the secretiveness of it all; the way everything was understood without being talked about.

There was still a lot of light left in the sky, and the night-black beach in an improbable moment had become a burning strip of silver. The woman turned to stare open-mouthed. 'Come,' she said as if she were dragging herself out of a dream. 'I'll show you around.'

But it was the man who did. He explained the difference between cutter rigs, gaff rigs and Bermudan rigs and why their boat was a Vancouver and not a Westerly or an Armagnac. All she remembered was that everything in their boat was tiny and perfect. There was a bed, a stove standing beside a shiny sink and what looked like a tiny fridge and toilet.

The woman had given her something to eat called pasta, a can of Coca-Cola, two lollipops, Chupa-Chups, whose wrapping she was going to keep, a big square of chocolate covered in gold paper and a packet of chewing gum.

They told her about places with pretty names like Albuquerque, Mississippi, Oklahoma and Ohio. They said they liked the way she talked, that she looked very strong for her age and she had the clearest eyes they'd ever seen. Sookramer had even fingered her hair and marvelled at its softness. She in turn had been allowed to touch the woman's and - although she did not show it - was surprised that it was not as soft as it appeared.

Missa Jonko took an apple, large as a fist and red like a ripe tomato, which he began peeling with the biggest knife she'd ever seen. He appeared not to be watching her but she knew he was and in her turn, she pretended not to observe him. And it was with something like mild shock that she saw him, with a flash of the wrist, drive the knife into the fruit and toss it in the water. 'Fetch it and its yours,' he grinned.

She leapt after it with alacrity and surfaced a few moments later with the impaled fruit.

'Great!' He brought his palms together thunderously. 'Now you got an apple.' Turning to Miss Sookramer, he said. 'I told you she's got talent.' And to prove that he was right he held up a silver coin and threw it a few yards beyond her.

She did not manage to retrieve it nor the others that he flung so casually overboard. When she surfaced, her face creased with disappointment, she saw that the man was smiling.

'The water flows that way,' he said, his hand sweeping in the general direction of where the lagoon opened out into the bay and then the world. 'You can't feel it but it flows. Always start a little way further up from where you want to go. Come tomorrow.'

'About this time,' the woman cut in gently, her eyes towards the houses on the hill.

'Yep!..and I'll teach you how to dive anywhere, for anything. I'm gonna make you famous. You know why? Because Susan and I, we think you're special.'

She realised the man meant what he said as soon as she swam over the following day, for he had a can of coins on deck. Again they'd drawn the boat closer to the mangroves. 'Y'know what's great about this game?' Missa Jonko laughed. 'I throw em, you git em, you keep em. Remember what I told you yesterday about starting further up? Here we go-oh!'

That was how, in the evenings that followed, she learnt to anticipate the dizzy spiralling of dimes, the direct plunge of large glass marbles with wondrously foliated irises, the slant of paper knives and nails, the somersault of tiny silver saucers, the twirl of metal rulers and whatever else the man decided to throw at her. And what made it all the more amazing was that Missa Jonko never seemed to run out of pretty things to toss. It was as if he'd conjured up these bright unsteady objects from his mind to do his personal bidding in the water.

The little cave she'd dug under the tuft of cus-cus grass below her cedar tree above The Silent became a bulging glittering nest. She now counted three penknives on which was written the word, 'Kiwi' in silver; a fingernail clip that was also a can opener; a tiny brass box with engravings of naked people that looked curiously flat against the metal; a silver ring with the head of a lion on the top; and the most treasured of them all, a round copper case full now with dozens of what the man called half-dollars and which were the most difficult to retrieve because he had ordered her to wait until he counted fifteen before she went after them.

The days, too, had assumed the glitter of these objects. Bright days in which she avoided the people who used the beach on evenings. She had developed what she imagined was a protective sheen around herself which guarded her from their stares, their silences, their words.

She'd done this right after Anna May had spoken to her. It was after her fourth visit to the boat. The woman had crooked a finger at her and Sienna had approached cautiously since there was no mistaking the tightness in Anna May's manner, which meant that what she was about to say was going to be very hurtful.

'What you doin on dem people boat? Eh? You know what yuh playin wid? Eh? You dunno is trouble dem people does bring? I wouldn let my Preeso spend five minutes on dat boat. But little girl like you, you across deh all evenin, every day. What yuh Tanty sayin bout all o dat? Eh? Is why I never like dat ooman. She too damn careless for me. If is somewhere you want to come when evenin come, come to my house. You kin help me do de washin up. You kin sweep mih yard. A little girl like you have good use. I know you strong. I does watch you. But dat boat, dem people! Is warn I warnin you.' And with that the woman had walked off muttering to herself.

That was why she decided never to see the stares, hear the words or heed anybody's crooked finger anymore.

If she didn't know better she might have believed that the man had overheard everything that Anna May told her because it was from that very day that his smiles were replaced by a curtness that seemed somehow more natural to him and which she did not mind because this persistent drill, this daily biddng to slip beneath the shadowy skirts of the lagoon, to retrieve and keep those pretty things had also brought a strange sobriety upon her.

Now she did the things Tan Lin asked her to do without complaining and Cedric's teasing no longer triggered the usual peppery outburst. In fact more than once he complained that she ignored him.

If Tan Lin had heard about or noticed her disappearances on evenings, she was saying nothing although a couple of nights before, believing that she was asleep, her aunt had brought the lamp down over her and moved it along her body slowly, the way a fisherman would check a craft for dents or weakened seams. Then with a smack of her lips she'd straightened up and left the room.

Sienna had already rehearsed the truth just in case she asked, anyway. She would say that Missa Jonko was teaching her to dive so that a man in America called Missa Olympic could judge her and tell her she was the greatest in the world. The presents she would get for that were made from proper gold too. But it meant a lot of practise. It meant diving deeper than anyone had gone before. It meant learning to place a hook around a ring on the box that Jonko had lowered to the bottom of The Silent. It meant understanding everything the man taught her the very first time because he did not like to repeat himself.

He would have her dive until the sky had drained itself of light and the water had become too dark for her to see what lay below. It was only then that he would allow her to dry out on that part of the deck he called the coach roof, while she answered Miss Sookramer's questions, her eyes fixed on the stone at her throat.

At first, the woman's gestures and expressions had been confusing, like some new road whose twists and turnings her feet could not anticipate. And so she would take the broad things: the show of teeth that meant a smile, the laugh that indicated ease, and of course the kindness in the voice that was always there; or the hurt that sat behind the calm whenever the man's impatience turned on her. She was the kind who liked to laugh though, and it was this that allowed Sienna to get past the constant questions, and the odd way she sometimes said things, to the feelings underneath.

A few days ago, in the middle of a laugh their eyes held briefly, a small silence descended upon them and they knew then that they had become friends.

'Are you coming tomorrow?'

It was Sookramer's way of telling her to leave. It was what she always said before lowering her voice and bringing her hand around her mouth. 'Can you bring me something green? Some leaves or flowers - anything, please?'

Sienna would not go home straight away. She made her way to the lip of the precipice above The Silent to watch the night creep in from the sea. She would watch the muted cabin lights come on and if it were one of those evenings when the air was very, very still, their voices would lift and drift upwards towards her. She would stay there until tiredness or night with a sudden, tropical chill that always took the strangers by surprise, drove them down below. The yellow lanterns would go out and it would be depthless-dark down there and very, very lonely.

ooooooo

It was their eleventh evening in The Silent and even Anna May seemed to have grown if not more tolerant then at least less concerned about her visits to the boat. Something else seemed to be bothering her. No one, the woman said, had ever known a yacht to remain so long in the Silent. Why de hell dey didn go back where dey come from? Missa Jonko had long since ceased to comment on her diving. In fact it had been some days since she'd heard him mention competing for Missa Olympics.

That evening, she'd slipped into the water, and after taking several turns at hooking up the rope to the ring on the box he'd lowered on the floor of the lagoon, he raised his arm, shouted something and sent what looked like a great silver plate skidding across the water. It was no more than a disappearing dazzle by the time she responded. She moved quickly but she found she could not keep up with the object's ghostlike plunge. She followed it though, even when she noticed a difference in the way the water felt, even when the cold began to curl itself around her and, like a giant living muscle, the ocean began to shrug her back. It was an odd sensation and she wasn't prepared for it. Nor was she prepared for the fright that flooded her senses.

She curved and headed upwards surfacing explosively, choked and mystified because for some reason the lagoon had lost its bottom. The strangeness did not stop there, for when she'd popped her head above the water she could have sworn she heard the woman's shout but when she blinked the water from her eyes, Sookramer was sitting at the front of the boat as relaxed as ever.

'I didn, I couldn,' she spluttered.

'Fergeddit,' Jonko laughed. 'Just an ashtray, that's all.'

'It didn have no bottom down dere... it.'

'Aww, c'maan, kiddy. I admit it. I been pushing you. Everybody gits tired. Tell you what, Susie's gonna make you some of that custard stuff you like and we'll fergeddit for the day. Okay Susie? Give her whatever she wants, she's earned it.'

It was too early to go home, or anywhere else for that matter. She was glad to see Jacko, struggling under the weight of a basketful of coralfish on the beach. She addressed him without pleasantry or protocol. 'How come de Silent have bottom one minute, an next minute it don't have none Missa Jacko?'

The man turned his head as much as the basket would allow him. Perhaps he had not forgiven her for keeping all his fish that last time, or perhaps the weight of the basket had put him in a bad mood but his mouth twisted itself around an obscenity before he rumbled, 'Whey's you manners! Whey you come from! What you talkin to me for! Go home y'hear me? Go home an keep yuh broad-mout' little backside quiet. It have more tings in dat water dan nobody round here don know nothing bout. GO!'

She waited the anger out. 'Tell me,' she muttered, her voice quiet and entreating.

'Leave me, girl. Is you flippin funeral you askin for!'

Because he hadn't answered her, she decided to swim back to Jonko's boat. She hadn't worked out exactly how she would ask him; she would perhaps put it the way she had put it to Jacko, not forgetting her manners this time. The ladder was still down and she clambered onto the craft, uncomfortably aware that she had never boarded without their invitation. Sookramer's shouting froze her. They must have heard her because there was a tumbling down below and then a sudden silence. Jonko emerged, grinning. The seagull's eyes were narrowed down and there was a frown above the smile. 'Forgot something?'

She shook her head, licked her lips to begin the question but he cut in pleasantly. 'Actually, I'm glad you came back. Got something for you.' His head popped down and up again. 'This - this is for you.'

She stared at the man dumbfounded. It was a pair of yellow flippers. New. And by the look of it, her size.

'Nice, huh? It's yours, but you'll have to leave it here. Of course you'll keep it when we leave.'

'Leave?' She stared at his face, the boat, then at the water.

'Didn't Susan tell you? Let's talk about it tomorrow. Okay?' She nodded. He pointed at the flippers. 'Leave them there. Tomorrow I'll show you how to use them. See yah.'

She clambered down the ladder noisily so that they could hear her leave.

Neither Jacko nor Jonko had answered her question; Jacko out of rage, Jonko out of an avoidance she could not understand.

She had no doubt that Sookramer would have told her what had suddenly become so important for her to know. Sookramer, whose scream she carried in her head now, whose blue-sad stare reminded her of that of the women of The Silent only theirs were darker and seemed to be fixed on things much, much further away. Sookramer, whose voice she knew she'd heard and which had died the instant it had taken her to clear the film of water from her eyes. Sookramer, on whose arms and back and legs the long, red marks she'd said the sun had burned there made a different kind of sense now.

She swam fast in the sleek and noiseless sideways manner that the man had taught her. She headed for The Mouth. There, with an almost experimental distraction, she allowed its pull to take hold of her, forcing herself to drift with it until she felt the silent, sucking cold. Then, with a violent flash of limbs, a sudden twist of rage that both surprised and pleased her, she pulled herself loose from its grip and headed for the beach.

She stared almost with a stranger's eyes at the little yacht, framed against the dark embrace of mangrove. Everything was quiet out there, even the gulls seemed to have vacated the sky and the whole world had turned a seashell pink. Silvery ribbons of clouds hung over the place where the sky curved down and melted with the water. For no reason she could identify, she suddenly felt like crying. Was snapped out of it when she heard the engine of Jonko's dinghy.

She watched it cut a frothing path along the edges of the lagoon. Soon it was heading out of the bay towards the grey smudge that was Krill Island and in no time at all it was a small dot on the darkening heave beyond.

She heard her name then, pronounced with the by-now-familiar drawl, which she used to find so pleasing. Sookramer, dripping and barefooted, was making her way over the stones which served as a jetty for boats and a place where the children caught whelks and harassed conga eels. She walked with the daintiness of one of those speckled long-legged birds that visited the lagoon during the Easter months. The girl did not look up. The woman lowered herself beside her. There was an aura to her, or rather an odour - a mild freshness - which Sienna could never decide whether she liked or disliked.

'I couldn't come up to see you, Millie. Not in the state I was in. Sorry. Hedgehog's gone over to one of your little islands. Left something out there.' She stretched out her feet and examined them. They were the colour of one of Tan Lin's loaves. The toes were long and pink like earthworms.

'What's it like up there?'

'Uh?'

'Up there where you live.'

'Dunno, we live up dere. Dat's all.'

The woman laughed. 'You make it sound like a stroll on the beach.' Still smiling she wriggled her toes, pulled her feet in and began picking at the nails. They were painted a silvery blue. She turned her eyes on Sienna, her forehead pleated in a tiny frown. 'I watch your shapes sometimes, moving against those fires in what I suppose is your front garden?'

Sienna, pretending to be fascinated by what the woman's hands were doing, did not respond.

Sookramer flung her hair back and released a long, hissing jet of air. 'Well, there is something terribly warm and close and unconnected about it. A bit like a dream I suppose, only you - you make it real. Those fires, is that what you cook on?'

'No,' she muttered. 'We just like fire.'

'How do you live? No I don't mean that; well not like that. What makes your people laugh? How do they love?' She paused over that, seemed very worried about something, and then she added smiling, 'I've heard it said that different people love differently, although John is one of those who don't believe that people can love at all.' She began laughing, the way cats mew, a soft high pitched sound. And then the blue eyes got darker, the lips tighter and somehow thinner. 'What frightens you, Sienna? I mean.' She brought her hands up to her face and stared thoughtfully at *Cincinnati Dreams*, now pink like the inside of a conch shell. 'I don't want to waste this chance.'

'You didn tell me dat y'all - y'all leaving.' Sienna spoke as if it had never occurred to her before. And it hadn't. Not really. Not until Jonko had said it. These people were like something she had wished for and had woken up one morning to find standing on the beach. Like a present. Presents did not go away. Presents were things you kept.

Sookramer pushed her hair back from her face and swung her head to face her. The hair flowed promptly back in place. Her eyes had gone a depthless amethyst. And she wasn't smiling now. 'We have to go. There's something he left back in St. Vincent. Thought he wouldn't need it. But he has to come back. He must.'

'You coming back with him?'

It seemed an eternity before she answered. 'Only if I, er, if I have to. If I have to protect you from him. He'll come back and he'll call you. He'll offer you more things and you'll come and do what he asks because, at the moment, that's what you want to do more than anything. He knows that. What he doesn't know is why. I'm not sure I know why either, but,' she rested speculative eyes on the girl, 'I suspect that it hasn't got a lot to do with us. Not all of it. That makes sense?'

'Lil bit,' she mumbled, herself sobered by Sue's sobriety. She thought she'd seen her thoughtful before, but not like this, not with this querying uncertainty.

Sienna fixed the stone at the base of her throat. 'He does beat you up.'

The woman sucked in her lower lip and stared across the water. Sienna could hear her breathing, soft like the way she spoke, like the way she walked and touched and laughed. Like the way she seemed to be with everything. Like she had imagined Lucille, alive and whole.

'Don't you have a single idea of what this might be all about?' The voice tightened and the woman swung round to face her. For some reason Sienna felt mildly chastised. She shifted her gaze to the red crabs that had surfaced on the sand, their yellow eyes like small revolving flames above their heads.

Sookramer was about to tell her bad things. Things she didn't want to hear. Everybody was like that. People started off by saying nice things and then as soon as a person began believing them they turned around and spoilt it.

Like that time Tan Lin had called her by those awful words, *Petit jamette laid!* She did not understand them, but coming from her aunt's mouth with that quiet sizzling violence, those words sounded like a curse. They seemed to carry the weight and sting of one. They were in fact, a couple of extra barbs on that nasty hook that people were so quick to string her on: the ugliness they reminded her of so often. The ugliness she had once offered Cedric all her food to deny, just once, for a moment, over dinner. And even then he could not bring himself to do it. 'Well, you not ugly,' he'd told her reaching for the plate. 'You more like a fella, dat's all.'

'I give you my food to tell me what I *is*, not what I is not!' And she'd snatched the plate of food back, which made him smile and lower his eyes.

Maybe all Sookramer and Jonko had told her about how good she was at diving, how nice they thought her teeth were, how quickly she'd learnt the things they'd shown her, maybe all of that hadn't been true.

'He does beat you up,' she repeated, her voice slightly more insistent.

'We fight - yes, more and more now - over you.'

Sienna's eyes widened on the woman's face.

'Look. You must not come back. You must stay away, d'you hear me?'

'Why?'

'Because it's wrong. Because we're strangers. Because you don't know us. Because it's, it's not a place for you.'

'Why?' Suddenly the hot-eyed clenching, the sudden fizz of irritation, which had never been necessary with these strangers, began to rise and clog her throat.

Sookramer's face and neck had reddened and Sienna had the odd sensation that the woman was about to cry.

'Because I - I do not want you to.'

'Missa Jonko want me to!' She was halfway to her feet when the woman's hand closed on her wrist with shocking strength. 'Sit down! And listen to me! I'm trying to tell you something. I'm trying to save your god damn life! This!' Her fingers traced a large, furious circle on the sand. 'This is your lagoon. How d'you call it? Never mind. This - can you guess what this is?'

Sienna squinted at the shape 'The boat....'

'Right.' Sookramer looked up briefly at the sea. 'Here - this is where he's had you diving.' She made a small circle near the boat. 'Have you noticed that its getting deeper all the time, that now you're almost doubling the depth you began with?'

The girl nodded.

'That's because he's shifting that boat every time.'

'I know.'

'You know!' The woman looked at her with wide, bright eyes. 'Then I shouldn't have to tell you that this is not about teaching you a better way to do anything. Right? I don't need to tell you that he's taking you closer to where he really wants you to go. Do you know where that is? Do you know what it's like down there?'

'Course - I been...'

'No you don't!' Sookramer's ferocity stunned her. With an urgent sweep of the hand, she cleared the drawing off the sand and began to draw again. She stopped abruptly and with a toss of her hair she looked up about her. The stone sparkled in the light like blue fire.

'Look up there. That tree, the one with all the flowers, d'you see that tree?'

She could have told the woman it was her tree. It stood a little way back from the edge of the cliff that dropped sharply down to the lagoon. She could even tell the woman the way the roots curled out of the soil like a tangle of brown eels and the secret hollow she had dug there for her things. Sookramer did not wait for a response.

'Now imagine the top of that tree is the surface of the water and the foot of it is the bottom. That's where you dive to normally. Now imagine you're swimming forward from the bottom of that tree. What happens?'

The girl looked up and then across to where Sookramer indicated and then she held the woman's gaze in terrified, tight-lipped wonderment. 'Dat - dat's why! It got another..'.

Sookramer nodded grimly. 'Yes - another bottom a little way further out. That bottom where you dive to is just the top of, well, a sort of precipice.'

'Deep - like a precipice?'

The woman nodded grimly. 'Like a precipice, except it's underwater. Although it is, well, put it this way: there are a couple of ledges, shelves, stairs - whatever you want to call them - on the way down. You can't get to the last, er, bottom. It's too deep, thank God for that. What's lost down there will stay lost. The weight of the water will kill you, anyway. There are eight boxes down there - on the first ledge - with rings on them. The sonuvabitch who dropped them there just dropped them in the wrong place.'

The girl held her breath. She remembered Mosan's words and the evening talk amongst the adults about the boats that passed and dropped crates of gin-an-whisky along the edges of Krill island for other boats that hauled them up at night.

In fact, Missa Jacko and his friends had gone one Low-Tide night and retrieved a dozen bottles for themselves. But never in their lagoon. 'Gin-an-whisky?' She exhaled.

'You're so god damn naive, you make me want to cry. In a few places less than a hundred miles from here some things are worth a lot of money. More money than you people here will ever earn from selling your bananas.'

'There's a little canvas bag down there weighted with lead. He didn't tell me it was there at first, and when he did last night he wouldn't tell me what's in it. Money, shit, ice - I don't know, I don't care, but he wants it more than all the rest. Enough to think your life is worth it. It's on the second ledge. After you place that hook around those boxes, he'll send you down there last. I know why he's gone this evening - the sonuvabitch. He's gone for grease - do I need to tell you why?'

The girl stared blankly at the blue stone.

'For the cold. At least you know that much. And then there is the pressure. You won't feel it straight away. We'll both be gone by then. But the cold and the weight of the water will hurt you. That..'. She waved tiredly at the sea, 'That's nothing. Down there it's a very different ocean.'

After a while she lost track of Sookramer's words, absorbed more by the sound of them, the way the woman wrapped her tongue around them, the emotions that they rode on - at once soft with rage and harshened by a frightening indignation - as if she were railing more against herself than Missa Jonko.

How, she wondered staring at the markings on the sand, how did they - strangers to her world in every way - how could they know so much more about her place than the very people who lived here?

The fact that they found it so easy to explain everything was as astonishing as the idea of a deeper drop, another bottom to their lagoon. Even the way Sookramer described what lay below the glittering heave they looked on every day held its own benumbing fascination: a different ocean.

It was as if in presenting it that way Sookramer was telling her something, not just about The Silent, but also about herself and her people. That there were other worlds around them, realities against which they rubbed each day without knowing they existed. And because they did not know, because they had not gone beyond the idle wondering, the short-lived pulse of a curiosity which they never gave themselves permission to pursue, because they did not know their place, it belonged less to them.

Awareness then was the beginning of a kind of ownership. A doorway to belonging. It came more as a feeling than an idea and when it did it felt whole and round and not at all uncomfortable. She blinked it back, swallowed hard on it lest the woman saw or sensed the change of mood in her.

And it was that mood that made her wonder with the same detachment with which she regarded the remains of some odd new creature or bit of flotsam on the sand; why would Jonko or any person for that matter want to do something like that to someone else? To call them nice names, smile with them, make them feel they were important; and then, by some means she did not fully comprehend, with that same smile, the same gestures of kindness, seek to make the sea destroy them?

She knew, as everyone else on The Silent did, that every time she turned her heels up at the sky there was no law that said that she would ever see the day again. That the ocean might simply decide to embrace her and not release her until it had drunk her breath and added her life to its own. But that awareness did not frighten her. It was not the same thing. Her people often said that no one could predict when the sea would take a life but what was certain though was that it would never waste it. With Jonko it was like showing her a room in her own house, which she had never known was there and then deciding to lock her up in it to die.

A question occurred to her, which she wanted to ask Sookramer, and she might have done so hadn't the woman still been speaking. 'One thing I've learnt about you, you're smarter than you're letting on. You're..' Sookramer's mouth stayed open. She reached under the nest of hair at the back of her neck and her fingers fumbled there. The silver chain cascaded like water into the palm of her hand and made an island of the blue stone. 'You like this, don't you? Take it. I - I have to go.' It slipped onto Sienna's knee, flowed down on the sand and settled at her instep. The girl picked it up, wide-eyed, speechless. She moved to hand it back. But her friend had scrambled to her feet.

'Go home,' she hissed. 'Go to your people and don't come near this place until we leave. Y'hear me! And - and for Gawd's sake don't tell him what I told you.'

And then she was running, her eyes not on the sand but on the boat approaching in the distance.

Later, she told herself that she did not have the time to tell Sookramer that it was not Jonko's boat because the woman was off the moment her eyes had fallen on the speck that had emerged from behind Krill Island. More truthfully though, Sookramer's terror had fascinated her. Fear was something she simply had not thought was possible with them.

How, she wondered idly, her eyes fixed on Mosan's approaching craft, how did Sookramer expect her to say anything to Jonko when she was supposed to keep away from him?

Missa Mosan did not greet her. With his usual deliberation he was trying to get his hand under the tail of a hefty tuna. This was a man, they said, who never sold the things he caught; who, by some baffling agreement with the sea, returned always with enough to feed his crowd of children even when the ocean offered nothing at all to others.

'Missa Mosan?'

'Yaas!'

'What is de deepest deep a pusson kin dive.'

'Deep? What deep?' He did not look at her. He was still working his hand under the fish.

'Deep Missa Mosan! Deep-deep-deep - where a pusson kin hardly see de bottom from de top.'

The man straightened up, began working his jaw, as if he were passing the idea around his mouth to get the exact taste of it.

'What kind o pusson?'

' A pusson like you. A pusson like anybody,' she replied, her eyes avoiding his.

'How deep is deep?'

'Deep,' she insisted. 'Like from de top o dat tree to halfway down de cliff.'

'Dat what dem askin you?' He was looking at her closely.

She frowned a quick denial. 'Is not dem dat askin nothin Missa Mosan, is jus know I want to know.'

He chewed some more. 'From dat tree up dere you say?'

She nodded.

This time his mouth clamped down on his thoughts deciding perhaps that what he'd tasted was not good at all. 'Not nice, not nice.' He muttered. 'Not nice at all! A dive like dat kin kill a man. I hear you hit de bottom of de Dredge?'

She nodded again.

'Dat what dem askin you? Dat why dem makin you skin kufum across dat water dere?'

'Dem teachin me to dive. Dem..'.

'Don't lie for me. Next ting you goin tell me is dem tryin to make de water wet!' He turned his back on her.

She watched him haul the small boat up the sand. There was something flat and angular about him that reminded her of those one-sided fish she often spotted on the sea floor. Even his head was like that, with hair like hers, scorched a rust-brown at the fringes by sun and salt. But it was his feet that fascinated her, narrow at the heels and flared like spatulas at the front. Feet that had the same compact toughness of his body and it was there she decided, thinking of the yellow flippers that Jonko had given her, it was in the size and shape of those amazing pair of feet that lay the secret of his diving. She looked down at her own feet and decided they were like his. Not as large, but that would come with time.

'Nobody in de worl kin dive like we. Cos nobody make to dive like we.' She said this finally, tentatively, without pride or gesture, like something that had just revealed itself to her. And he took it the way she meant it. The man swivelled his head around and a broad surprised smile pleated his face. 'When dey leavin? Cos dem have to leave here soon.'

She realised that he too had been counting the days. He too had been having thoughts about Sookramer and Jonko.

'Tonight, p'raps tomorrow.' She shrugged. 'It don't matter.'

She could not decide whether it was a cough or curse that issued from Mosan's mouth. Nor was she sure about the look he gave her. He turned to squint speculatively at the tree above the lagoon. Again he turned his back on her. His words came faltering and subdued. 'If was me, if is have I have to go. I goin to tek it fast.'

He seemed taken by his own idea. He chewed on it furiously for a while and then he straightened up and fixed the tree. 'Speed, speed is what is nerecerry for dis kind o dangerousness, cos is dangerousness I call dat. An before I go; before I decide to play rummy wid mih life for nothing, I'll tell meself, I'll say, 'Mosan don ferget to tek your time comin up. Strong as de water is, cold as it is down dere, hurt as mih chest goin be hurtin, bustin as mih lungs goin be bustin, I have to come up slow. Becos comin up fast kin leave ah whole heap o bubble in yuh blood an when it reach yuh heart.' He brought his palms together with a sudden thunder-clap that shook her to the core.

'What time o day a pusson might be thinkin bout?' He threw a worried glance not at her but at the sea.

'Dunno - no time, Missa Mosan. I was only askin. I was.'

'Mornin!' He growled. 'Early as a pusson kin make it. Before de sun come up an hit de water. Ain't got no tide dat

time. De water don't wake up yet. It have to be early mornin.'
He looked at the sea as if seeking approbation for those words,
took up his crocus bag and swung the tuna off the sand.

He was half way up the hill before he checked his stride.
'Once, Miss Lady! Jus once.' He shouted without turning.
'Yooman-been not make to do dat twice. Jus once - o else.' He
did not say the rest but that clap of his hands still echoed in
her head and without realising it, she nodded.

ooooooo

She never spoke about what happened afterwards and the
little that The Silent learned came from the mouths of those
who went out hours before the stirring of the gulls, when
morning was still a faint suggestion against a sky the colour
of mud-soaked canvas. Those who boasted eyes that could
spot the markings on a gull's wing in the middle of a squall
claimed they saw the flash of yellow flippers in the lagoon
near the boat. It was something their minds rejected at the
time since it fitted into nothing a straight-thinking person
expected.

What was certain was the emergence of the girl, bone-
soaked and shivering, from somewhere near the tree above
the lagoon. The women claimed that it was the chattering of
her teeth that had made them lift their heads from their
breakfast fires in the yard. And it was the oddness of the sight
of her, more shape than substance in that early morning, that
had turned their eyes down towards the beach a hundred
yards or so at the bottom of the dry, white hill of cactus and
mint grass. There, they too spotted the yellow flippers
arranged side by side on the sand like a pair of outlandish
parrot fish.

She'd gone into the house, stripped and pulled around
herself every spare bit of dry clothing she could lay her hands
on, including Cedric's underpants. And then she had laid

herself down on the floor and sank into a kind of darkness which they all agreed, was nearer death than sleep.

They knew it as The Chill, an illness that was as hard-to-come-by as a queenshell. A person recognised it by the pallor of the skin and the coldness that seemed to surface from the bones and settle in a kind of sweat there.

The 'sleep' lasted four days. Tan Lin's candlelight inspection of her body had not delivered any answers. If Sienna had been tampered with, she said, it was in a way that went beyond her understanding.

By then the whiteman's boat like all the other boats that had come before had left.

And when Sienna came out of it, with her eyes still turned in on the ocean from which she had just emerged - reluctantly it seemed - she smiled as if she had surfaced with some secret. And from then they could not keep her inside the house. She sought light and air greedily like a baby seeking milk. So that The Silent was moved to say that she was born again. That the thing that had brought her back that morning all wet and trembling had taken away a life from her and replaced it with a new one.

Cedric told her about the boat leaving, less intrigued by her friendship with the strangers than the odd sight of a woman at the prow, looking up at them, then across at the yellow flippers on the beach, her blue dress fluttering in the wind like that ill-fitting garment she'd sewn for Lucille, her face as pale and expressionless as an early morning moon. That, he told her, was two days before a couple of big grey boats with bright disturbing lights arrived and began circling The Silent.

The flippers were no longer where she'd left them after she'd swum back to the beach, emptied the heavy little canvas bag and slipped into the sea again, this time to toss the empty sack on deck where she thought Sookramer ought to see it since mornings, she was always first to come up from below.

Sienna imagined the white trail that the boat would have made all the way out past Krill island and Sookramer, sad and smiling at the prow, casting a last glass-blue stare at the houses and the beach. Surprisingly, the sense of abandonment she had anticipated was not there.

Indeed The Silent was empty as if they had never come.

Chirren

It so happen that the prison I was working in was about fifty yards or so above the women own and believe me, is know them woman did know that. They used to dance for the fellas sometimes. Never looking up of course because looking up while they dancing was like extra cruelty and provocation. Was like offering them fellas something they couldn't really have. Yunno that calypso: *A twist o she waist an a wink from she face was what start de riot?* Well I swear the fella who make that one up must have been inside once.

Dancing in the yard was against the regulations anyway, but you know how blackooman stop. You can't stop them. When you think you stop them, is start them getting ready to start. Sometimes one of them lift she hand and make a kind of S with she body, cos she know them fellas was up there looking down from every crack they could find in the wall. One little movement and just like that, she subvert the whole establishment. Just like that, she mash up man sleep. Just like that she full up them fellas night time with a whole heap of discontentment.

And that was nothing compare to when the long-hair one - the troublemaker name Sinty - expose a thigh or let go one of them fancy-laugh, deliberate, or pull all of them together in one movement and pretend is for sheself that she behaving rude so. Jeezas! When night come, us warders had to caulk we ears with fist because them fellas making so much noise.

But wasn't that what nearly cause the riot.

The Chief down there was a woman name Miss Sharbellows who was always experimenting with ideas she pick up from Yourope. We Chief used to tell we that the woman was chupid because Youropean criminal commit much worser crime than we but them does do it with refinement. We criminal was more harden, that was all; and is because we have such poor-quality criminal that Sharbellows experiment was bound to fail.

Anyway, it happen one morning after a really bad night because Skinnit, the quiet babyface one with the glasses - who I been reliably informed, was writing a book in secret - that young fella take a bed sheet to he neck and we had to lift him down.

Them kind of incident always leave a little bit of bad mood afterwards so we was extra careful to keep a eye on everybody over breakfast. Them fellas was eating, slow and contemplative, when sudden so, the grumbling and plate-knocking stop, an all of dem lookup as if them hear the Holy Ghost. I hear it too, like a flock of seagull in the distance. I hear it and I shift and lift my gun and watch the others who was keeping duty with me. I watch them do the same because I have to say that is a very funny feeling you does get when every thief, wife-beater and murderer in the land fix he eye on you. Is not a nice feeling you does get at all, at all, at all.

One thing for sure though! We know the drill: Step One, you lift your rifle, grab the bolt and snap it back. It have many a time that I stop a fight or a half-crazy fella with that sound alone. But it didn't work this time, so I realise was serious trouble coming.

'Chirren!' somebody shout. 'Is chilren!'

They was through the door and heading for the yard before we could even think of Step Two. In fact when my gun shoot off in the air, it was me myself it frighten because was the first time I ever reach as far as Step Two. Them fellas didn't hear it! Serious! They didn't hear it at all. Or maybe they hear it and they didn't care. Or maybe they care but they didn't want to hear it. I don't know. What I know was that by the time we gather forces and head out for the yard together, frighten as hell but well prepare for Step Three, they was climbing up the fence. They was elbowing one another. They was jostling and climbing one on top the other. They was making nuff noise

So I point the rifle in the air like regulation require and order them to freeze. They hear us this time. I sure they hear us because all of them turn round and look at we like if we stupid, like we was mad, like we gone bazodi or something, like we eat boli guts. Like we was ordering a river to go back up the hill it just come down. There was this big fella, government man he used to be before all that bloodshed happen, who, since they bring back the gallows in Trinidad was more fraid to dead than anybody else. Even he, he look at Chief an show him all he teeth, 'Comrade,' he say, 'You hear what we hearing down there? You hear that?'

By that time the one who they call Machiavelli manage to get as far up as the spikes and barbwire on top the wall. He was up there ignoring them cut on he hand, ignoring the Chief who was threatening to shoot him down. 'I see dem, I see dem. I see dem.' Was all he shouting. 'Is dem I see - I see dem.' And it take a little time before we realise that it was not laugh that he was laughing. After a while he come down quiet and went straight back to the Mess.

It get so quiet I could hear meself sweating as we watch them fellas make way for each other. Help each other go up and come down, go up and come down, one by one, till everybody get a good look over that wall. In fact I tell meself that it was a good thing that *we was* so dam frighten we forget to shoot.

I was the last to look. I didn't have to, I not even sure I did want to, but I got proper training in Barbados. Is in Barbados I learn that in the eventuality of riot or disturbance, or distress I must first locate the source and neutralise it.

Well, I didn't see no source down there. All I see was them women with their little children, inspecting them, passing their finger through their hair, smelling them, skinning back their eyelid, wiping their face with the tail of their frock, wrapping themself around them; letting them go and grabbing them back fast-fast, yunno. The kind of foolishness that only ooman does want to do.

Deliverance

For Esau

He could laugh at them as long and loud as he pleased, now that he had made his mind up.He'd finally resigned himself to the fact that neither doctors nor the foul-smelling sap of herbs could cure him. And there was another nasty truth: despite himself, despite his daily almost frantic dips in the sea and the layers of liniment he used to seal the wound below his ankle, he stank. It had taken a lot out of him to admit that, a fact that was as offensive to him as it was to the people who shunned him. But he'd finally found, if not the answer, then at least the promise of a cure.

The sore had aged him, sapped his strength and made an old man of him before his time. But Osun's vision, for it was more substantial than a dream, else why would it come to him so regularly and in such detail? His vision had revealed to him that the dolphin, the white one with the eyes like flames in her head could heal him.

She came again last night, not surrounded by the others this time, but alone, and revealed some very important things to him. He knew exactly where to find her now. And, not only had she promised him a cure - no, sir - she was offering him something even better if he followed her. A cleansing, that was what she'd promised him.

If the other dolphins, the ones that carried her sometimes, did not come with her last night, he thought, it was because they were not important. Only the albino - the white one - could cure the flesh of a foot gone bad on him. Only she could make him whole again. The dolphin had also understood that this was not a curse he'd deliberately called upon himself.

Who would believe that it was just a scratch at first, a tiny abrasion made by the tip of his harpoon a year ago? He'd ignored it, expecting the curative powers of the sea to heal it. Not an unreasonable expectation since all his life the sea had licked the cuts and bruises of the village, restoring and smoothing them over as naturally as it did the marks their feet left each day on the sand.

But salt and sun had not worked their miracle for him this time.

Skido was the only person prepared at least, to listen to him talk about the dolphins; the only person prepared to talk to him at all now. The others did not care; or perhaps his presence offended them so much they chose to keep well away from him. But the old man, those strangely depthless eyes of his fixed on Osun's face, never seemed to tire of him talking about the dream. Well, not until a couple of weeks ago. Then, there was something different about the way the old man listened.

'I see her, Missa Skid. White like god mek cloud. As if she was tellin me where to come to meet her so she kin cure this foot o mine.'

'Meet her where, Osun?'

'Past Dog Reef, sir. Past..'.

'Past Dog Reef is De Gate, sonny and De Gate is hell.'

'I know, sir. Past all that. Even past Gull Island.'

'Past all that you find nothing. Only water and wind and storm and - what de hell de matter with you, anyway! Like that bad-foot make you crazy, o something? Or...' The old man leaned very close to his face, 'is like you trying to say something so - so - flippin heavy, you kin only talk 'bout it to me in parables.'

'You can't call something, nothing, sir.' Osun made his words as clear and deliberate as he could, feeling very good because for the first time he felt self-assured enough to return Skido's gaze. 'Becos water, wind and storm is something. And if that is where she want to tek me to cure me of dis stink, then is go I gotta go. Not so?'

'You go, you never come back. You go searchin for any kind o white dolphin - especially white dolphin! Cross dat bad ocean water north o here, you never come back. Y'hear me? You die.'

'No I can't, becos she tell me...'

'You die, Osun! Nobody never go north o here, this time o year. And you know s'well as de rest of us dat is two weeks since the radio been predictin storm. You even think o trying it and dat sea swallow you up and spit your little magga-bone arse out on some bird-shit island somewhere where nobody can't find you. S'only a dream! God never mek no dolphin white all over; not de kind o white you talk to me about.

Dolphin is de colour o deep-water. I see blue ones, black ones, brown ones, even grey ones. But nobody never see no white dolphin dat shine like you say it shine, 'ceptin in de mind. Dat's not no dolphin, sonny - dat's de devil calling you, o your conscience. O both.'

'No! S'more dan dat, sir.'

Skido didn't want to hear more. Muttering, he pushed himself off the sand, dusted the seat of his trousers and walked off to the northern end of the bay.

The old man had avoided him ever since.

Still, Osun sighed, he ought to feel better now. He could allow himself to laugh because last night the answer had presented itself to him as plain as day. Osun closed his eyes.

From the cot where he lay, he listened to the humming, buzzing voices in the room next door.

The voices came in snatches; the high nasal tone of his niece and the strangely resonant bass of her companion. These days the two talked as if he were not there. He tried to remain quiet, to blank his mind but could not prevent his heart from thumping painfully at the words that came in fragments through the shaky, half-rotten walls of the house.

Edmund Hill. The Red House. Easier. The gov'ment.

He felt the sharp, unpleasant shock of fear run through him. The tension from listening hard had begun to make his head heavy. She had never talked like that before.

He'd detected a slight edge of uncertainty in the woman's voice, a kind of quiet desperation, a querulous seeking for assurance.

Nothin to shame for, eh? Not as bad as before. Better now, not so?

Osun allowed the words to sink like pebbles down the very deep pool that he imagined was his mind. These days he thought of himself, or rather parts of himself, in very strange ways. Sometimes his body was a sea-snake, the type that fed off the floor of the ocean. Or, in moments of depression or uncertainty he was all the old and soggy things the sea threw up on the beach just outside his niece's house.

A burden. That was what she said he was now. A burden.

She had become more fretful since the man arrived, more on edge with everybody. Still, if he were to be completely honest she seemed happier than he could ever remember her. But it was a happiness she reserved only for herself and the tall, sober-faced young man who had taken an instant dislike to him. Nesthia was quicker now to remind Osun of the effort it took to maintain him.

Her complaining subsided to something more internal, a slow and laboured sighing that grew deeper and more prolonged, in marked contrast to the man's short, deep-chested grunts.

He lay quiet, that strange feeling beginning to grow on him again, the tightening in his gut of anticipation tinged with fear that used to flow through him just before he stepped into his boat and headed for the distant threat of the horizon.

Osun was certain of one thing: he was not going to sit and rot the rest of his life away in a mad house or in a pauper's home on Edmund Hill. Everybody had heard about the Red House: the stink, the decay, the dying and the dead. He would not allow Nesthia, or rather her new man through her, to choose this shameful fate for him.

Osun shifted his weight on the small bed, ignoring Nesthia's and whatever-his-name's noisy commotion. They go on like that, he thought sourly, they would get more than the child they were trying for.

A large spider was slowly suspending itself from the dirty ceiling. It hung on a thread so fine it seemed to be afloat on an ocean of air.

A sharp laugh from outside cut through his concentration. His eyes strayed across the room, resting on the dirty board walls with its cardboard patches and the half-broken ugliness of chairs and table.

He wriggled his toes; studied them. They were long and bony but still strong. The old muscles were weaker but still there. His bones stood out against his skin now, but no fat. He smiled, looked sharply around as if he had let fall a clue to some very personal secret.

It had to be tonight. This night. It occurred to him that he was prepared, had in fact been waiting all these weeks for the moon.

It had gone quiet in the room next door. Osun rolled off the bed. He had already selected the boat that he was going to use. Had watched Chadoo prepare it for the trip out every morning at five o'clock exactly, watched him draw the heavy harpoon in and lay it carefully along the belly of the craft, the awesome steel of its barbed end pointing backwards towards the stern. The man would lay the long oars carefully beside the weapon before entering her. And then, heart racing, he would watch him, and his son, lift and fit the long white mast from which the single sail of pure black canvas would spread out so magnificently against the sky.

The craft was painted blue-grey, white and yellow, the colour of sky and clouds and sun and, yes, deep-water fish. Lean like a barracuda and with the impatience of a horse, it was easily the sleekest boat anyone had ever seen.

It had taken Chadoo three years to build that boat. Might have taken another man six months, but Chadoo had been born with shortened forearms and hands turned out like flippers. No-one believed that he could do it. Notwithstanding that, the little man had taught himself to hold a hammer with the crook of his arm and wield it more accurately than any person alive. Even then, Osun reflected, he might have finished his boat in a year or for the latest, eighteen months, but this was the work of a man too obsessed with his own imperfection to build an ordinary craft. Three years later, when he stepped back to look at his work, Chadoo saw that he had fashioned something after the image and likeness of his own inside-self. The most perfect boat on earth. Balanced beyond belief, it was large enough for deep-sea fishing but smaller than the twenty-footers in the bay since it was made to the measure of Chadoo's own stunted body.

So if Chadoo treated his boat like a man would do a horse, Osun felt he understood. When he scrubbed its painted sides each evening after a hard day's work, patted the nodding prow and addressed it by the name he had given it as soon as it was finished, Osun knew that the exchange was real. There was, for anyone who cared to watch, a shared understanding between *Deliverance* and her maker.

Lord ha Mercy, what a name for a boat! *Deliverance!*

Evenings, Chadoo never brought her up on the sand. With a long, heavy rope he'd ring-bolted against the sternpost, he would lead *Deliverance* and tether her against the trunk of the largest sea grape tree on the beach. Osun had studied that boat until its every line had become as familiar to him as his own body.

He had forced himself to eat well; even when it meant swallowing his pride and going down to the beach to beg for a handful of sprat or the odd fish head that he'd roasted on the sand or in his niece's coal-pot. If there was no offering of fish, he spent all evening combing the rocks on the southern end of the bay for whelks. He wasted nothing.

There was a small parcel of jack-fish and red snappers that he had salted, dried and then baked, hidden deep in the sand between the roots of the grape tree nearest their house.

Now he felt ready for anything.

The sun was already a rusting coin rolling down the back of the sky. The last of the buses from St. George's were screaming through the village, heading for the northernmost towns, Victoria and Sauteurs.

Half past six.

Already mosquitoes were rising in swarms from the mangrove swamp near the beach. The boats were coming in, engines throbbing throatily through the thick evening silence. He used to be part of the great line of incoming boats that pleated the water silver every evening, stretching all the way back towards the white, thundering edge of Dog Reef.

It felt better standing apart today: not pottering about the nets, head bent under the humiliating scrutiny of hardier, healthier men; not fighting his own body as he added his feebleness to the hauling up of boats from the water's edge to the shelter of the grape trees. He used to do it because he needed the poor reward of fish, thanklessly given later, after the men had sorted the best of the catch for themselves.

Jacob Ross

Chadoo walked past him, grunted a brief greeting. But Osun did not hear the man. His eyes were mirrors reflecting the flight of gulls over the restless water. Gulls. They were always beautiful to watch. Made for perfect flight. It made a person want to weep just watching them plunge, beak first, into the glowing water and then rise hard and fast as they shook the liquid salt and sunlight off their wings.

Voices cut rudely through his muse. The last of the men, loaded with fishing gear, trailed off the beach towards home and their women.

Night rolled in quickly. Night and the tide.

This being the hurricane season, most of the boats had been beached and secured against the trunks of the trees with thick ropes. The rest were left lying near the shore. If a storm stirred, these would be the first to be taken by the sea.

'Osun!'

He ignored his niece's voice. Now the beach lay pale and lifeless in the decaying evening light. Red crabs hung tensely over the gaping mouths of their holes.

'Ooo-sun!'

He felt alone.

'Osun!'

'Yaaar!'

'I callin you. You don't hear me callin you? How much time I mus stand up here callin you? I flippin tired o callin you! I can't afford to continue callin you for no food. An besides you does never answer when I callin you.'

'Awwright!' His mouth watered at the thought of food. Osun looked up expectantly at the foothills, breathed long and hard as he glimpsed the cold white eye of the moon just above the peaks of the Belvidere. Night had fallen about him like a stone.

ooooooo

70

It must have been past midnight. Both feet drawn up, eyes wide, his whole body was concentrated on the sounds in the other room. For the umpteenth time, Osun flicked his tongue across his lips - a nervous reaction that irritated him because he could not control it. He resented the tightness in his throat and the heaviness of his own heartbeat.

Edging off the bed was a slow, painstaking process. He had to be careful not to hurt his foot. He began to move the moment he heard the rustle of bed clothes and the heavy roll of bodies in the other room. He kept his eyes on the door. The bolt slid easily back under the large spider that was his hand.

The door grated, he froze, listened to the drawn-out sighs, the heavy breathing in the other room and grinned maliciously as he stepped out into the naked night.

The moon had grown. It hung full and low and heavy above the bay. And stars, numberless, Lordy! stretching beyond vision, beyond hope.

Used to be times when he thought of them as tears scattered on a black face. The white beach was strangely luminous against the darkness. Osun laughed a real laugh. He hadn't laughed like that in a long time. Years.

A low breeze tugged at his shirt. He chanced a glance at the sleeping houses framed darkly against the coconut palms and grape trees. Seized by a sudden fit of urgency he hobbled into the water, feverishly lifting the anchor of the boat and pushing Chadoo's craft a few yards further out.

The food! He had forgotten the food. Wouldn't survive without the food. Knee-deep in water, he ignored the pain in his ankle and pushed himself back towards the shore. If anyone was up, they would surely hear the racket he was making. Past caring, Osun dug the sand beneath the tree, his hands quick and crab-like. A satisfied grunt and he was off his knees, hopping once more towards the boats, frightened now because he noticed that where his room had been dark a moment ago, there was now the flickering light of a lamp. He thought he heard the man's deep grumble.

The door! He had not closed it. The draught must have roused the two, made them suspicious.

He managed to get the mast up by the time he heard the woman shout his name; fought with the sail wrapped and roped around the tall, beautifully cut and smoothed mapou pole. Slowly, the black sheet of canvas gave beneath his fingers and with an impatient flapping protest it opened itself up, seeking wind.

Osun thought he heard his name a second time, a man's grating cough, footsteps on the sand. He was hoping to God they hadn't seen him. Mercifully, the sail had found the slight night-breeze and stuffed itself a cheekful. Sweating and cursing the tremors, he guided the craft past the sleeping boats. The breeze became slightly stronger a few yards further out and the craft responded instantly, her hull already beginning the long and sibilant gossiping with the waves that was as distinctive as a signature to every boat. It was a sound that never ceased to thrill him.

It could have been his mind - the sudden dizzying flush of some deeply thrilling thing - that made him momentarily lose his sense of himself and where he was. An illusion that gave an odd metallic fluorescence to the water, as if the sea was the source of its own luminescence. It could have been that, and the eagerness of the vessel he'd just mounted which induced in him, this pleasantly unsettling sensation of slipping away on light.

Or perhaps it was real. *Deliverance* was actually taking him away on a glimmering ocean.

Osun turned his face up to the moon and laughed.

Behind, there were lights in doorways now - bottle torches whose erratic flames gave exaggerated life to shadows and distorted the dark even from this distance. Perhaps they did not see him yet? A black sail against a night sky was as good as not being there at all. Who would expect him to go out to sea this time of night? In this, the Hurricane Season. And what if they knew that he was heading north, as north as any man could go! Already the boat was bucking like a thing alive.

He felt excited. Tense, but unafraid.

Past Dog Reef the sea was a frenzy of white, rolling water, so bloated with indigestion from the bits of the world it had swallowed up, it threw them up on every bit of land it touched. But the sea, as his father used to tell him, was there for just one thing: to reclaim the earth. And long before Judgement Day arrived, the sea was going to have its way.

Come morning, they would pursue him. Osun was sure of that. They would come after him with those new boats, those ugly, noisy things with big engines. That was why he'd chosen this night. Tonight, at this hour there was not a man who would leave the warmth of his woman, the comfort of his house for the open sea.

Only Chadoo's oldest son - the reckless one - would want to come after him but the little man would never allow him to.

Already he was feeling the heavier toss and tug of the water as he left the shelter of the bay and rounded Short Horn.

Once again Osun thought he heard his name across the water, but it came as a sigh this time -the murmur of wind on waves, and it was so far away, anyway, he could easily be wrong.

The whole island would be alerted. They would be afraid for him, and marvel at his courage even while they prayed for him. His name would be on the radio, his picture in the papers. His real name - not Osun - but his long and full and proper name as his mother had baptised him: Osunyin Ignatius Ezekiel Frazier was going to be in everybody's mouth. The boats in the village would be leaving by the first light of morning. He was also sure of that. The police may even join the search.

He sent a spurt of spittle in a glistening arc across the water, chuckling hoarsely as it lost itself in the restless anonymity of the dark.

The craft leaned hard right, shuddering with the force of a new wind, a colder, harder wind that pounded his exposed chest. Laughing, the tiller firmly in his right hand, Osun threw his weight the other way and *Deliverance* responded instantly, steadying itself, the sail pregnant to the point of bursting.

Boiler Reef came up, a thunderous, frothing succession of breakers, writhing high and white beneath the wet moon.

Close! Too close! Girl you taking me too close!

Someone had told him once that Boiler Reef was where the island had decided to make its last, defiant stand against the all-consuming sea. Now staring across there it was easy to believe. Osun closed his eyes against the storm of spray, the better to feel the craft and struggle with it around the enormous suck and tug of waves.

Too flippin welly close. Cheezan bread! Too close!

He was soaked and slightly shaken when they emerged, but free. Truly free. Free of the land. All there was before him now was the rolling ocean, the big, wide, open ocean and tomorrow.

Tomorrow? What the hell did he mean by that? The notion had popped up unexpectedly and completed the thought for him. And then he grinned because it suddenly made sense. The boats with the big engines that would be coming after him at the crack of dawn had to do with the day ahead, the next day. But not tomorrow. Even if they caught him, brought him back and dumped him dried out and gulping on the beach back there, they would still be part of what he'd left behind.

Osun laughed again, convinced that some very important, elemental code had just been revealed to him, something as vital as water, as necessary as hope. Tomorrow. He savoured the thought because it had crystallised into something very hard and stable in his mind. Tomorrow was wherever *Deliverance* was taking him.

Morning was a feeling first. Little signs: the slight shift of wind in the sail, the changing tug of tide and the nature of the light down the edges of the sky. That and something else in the wind. The smell of it, a sharper, fresher quality that only the morning had. Time flowed by. Time was water slipping past the boat.

His thoughts were replaced by a vague urgency, a quiet presentiment which, try as he might and despite a sudden overwhelming feeling of drowsiness, he could not shake off. He had not slept, not properly; not only last night but the night before and the night before that. He thought that he might find some quiet water further on, let the boat drift there a while and well - just, well - doze off a bit.

Still fighting the cobwebs in his mind, Osun closed his eyes.

It was not until his boat was caught between two receding waves that he remembered The Gate. He leaned hard on the tiller, throwing all of his weight sideways, risking everything. The terrible concussive boom two hundred feet away hurt his eardrums and vibrated the craft. *Deliverance* slipped sideways down a mountain, her sails gone limp for the first time. Osun screamed because an oar had slipped and struck his foot, screamed the long fall down while he fought to right *Deliverance*. The craft, protesting against the effort, was straining hard against the murderous drag, her mast so low now, it was almost touching the water.

Another boat would have given up, capsized and perished there with him in the clutch of a ripping headwind where the currents of two great oceans crossed and clashed in a raging hell of water. He'd heard stories of bigger vessels that had gone that way, even ships, spat up eventually on some distant shore near Venezuela or some other country far beyond. But Chadoo's craft, running on its side, keel turned up almost to the sky, began the long and terrifying climb with him.

For the second time *Deliverance* delivered him and he thanked her fervently as he looked back, safe now, at the great heaving walls of grey, whose tops glinted like steel in the half-born day. Even from here the boat was still tossing and shuddering. Some fool, he thought, had named this hell hole, Paradise. God! What a name for the devil's own playground.

Old Man Tigga, he remembered, was the first to rename it The Gate. Just that. And when he'd chosen to end it there, deliberately, Osun, like the rest of the village understood then why The Gate was more appropriate. That was Tigga's way out. His chosen exit from a life that no longer held any interest or meaning for him because he'd grown too old to lift an oar.

The fact that Osun had gone so close had shaken him. Perhaps he had fallen asleep even while he was thinking that he needed to? Perhaps. He became frightened when he thought of it. It was no ordinary fear either because Paradise had haunted him in dreams. Terrified him. The nights, God, the nights when his woman, Lisa, had to drive the terror away with her warmth.

Below those waves there was something, something deep and dark and unapproachable; for no ordinary reef or rock could take that pounding. Whatever lay below that raging circle of water had a lasting hold on him. There was a time when he had tried to kill his fear by coming out here alone to the very edge of the fretful water, willing the glass-green hills to freeze so that he could see what lay below them. And the waves would even seem to oblige him - to pause ever so slightly before their rippling tops curled down and shattered his hopes with them. He felt weak and unhappy afterwards. Like nothing.

God! How it used to frighten him. The dreams. And the miserable nights with Lisa talking to him, Lisa rocking his wet head in her small hands. Lisa loving him. Lisa.

Osun turned the name over in his mind, trying to find her face, to add flesh and form to the one name that memory, in order to protect itself from pain had until now, buried somewhere in the backwaters of his mind. It was all so confusing, trying to picture Lisa, shuffling through the faces of the women that had shared his life, rejecting them, shuffling again, barely conscious of the boat slipping up and down the rolling sea.

Osun sat in a living dream, forcing himself to remember his woman as she was before she left him. He sat perfectly still staring patiently before him until she came, her image sharp and clear.

Lisa. There! Standing in his doorway, smiling that quiet, whimsical smile of hers, clean and small like a bird.

'Lisa,' he whispered, reaching out for her. The wind blew the breath of morning in his face, and his woman's name, made warm and soft and deep with feeling came drifting back to him.

'Lisa?'

Deliverance headed for the brightening sky.

Gull Island came up in a grey haze. The cold light of the early day and a hard, insistent breeze had dragged him out of his dreaming. Osun felt the rough fingers of hunger tighten in his stomach. The dried fish and water tasted raw. It occurred to him that he should occupy himself. The big harpoon lay at his feet. He measured it with his eyes; decided that he could throw it if he had to. He might not need the harpoon though. It was the big fishing line -the king line - that mattered. That was where the battle and the sweat and the danger lay. It was lying in thick coils in the bow, fathoms deep. The giant hook - the hidden fang to this great snake was buried somewhere in the centre.

He wondered how Chadoo ever used them, that and the harpoon, and remembered that he never did until his son had joined him on the sea a couple of years ago. Osun glowered at his foot. Used to be a time when no man or woman on earth could run a line like him. They called him King then - King of the king line - because he could haul anything out of the ocean: tunas and sharks and blue marlins that unfurled their fins like sails and fought the hook like the gods they were, the great blue gods of salt and water.

Sometimes it saddened him to bring them in.

The boat slid quietly into the small bay where heaps of rock edged down to the water. Through the morning haze, he saw the gulls wheeling in their thousands. The air vibrated with their cries. He had never seen so many gulls in one place before. Osun found the small line under the seat. He wanted bait for the king line. A bit of dried fish stuck at the end of the small hook was enough to attract the small black fish that lived off the mud of the sea-floor close to land. He caught one and it was easy afterwards. The flesh of the freshly caught fish, stripped and impaled on the hook, was enough to catch as many as he wanted.

His anxiety had not left him. Osun kept glancing around at the rim of the sky. The Gate was way off in the distance, a violent cloud of white that reached all the way up to the heavens. Its roar was faint on the wind but still frightening. Although he expected them, his heart began to race when he saw the boats. They were a long line against the horizon, tiny against the vast backdrop of sky and clouds. The sun, throwing its first bright blades across the water, struck the sails and lit them up. Osun used the oars to slip out of the bay, pausing to give *Deliverance* sail on the other side of the island.

Gull Island disappeared slowly behind him, a strange, barren place infested with giant cacti, mammoth stones and the great rusting metal tanks once used to melt the fat of whales. Something in him was afraid to lose the assuring sight of the island for it marked the boundary past which no fisherman would go.

The whole world knew that what lay beyond was more than ocean. After Gull Island was the straight, grey threat of uncertainty and the vast, tossing eternity of dark water. Of boundary-lessness.

Then so be it, he laughed. *Deliverance* would take him out there - to nowhere if need be - because that was where the dolphin said she wanted him.

Nothing around him now but sea. A wet desert. Now and then a gull would speck the hot bowl of the sky. The heavy line trailed fathoms deep behind the boat. What remained of it was secured against the keelson - the very spine of the craft - with Chadoo's own invention - a cross between a block and tackle and a rigging screw. Now and then he inspected it or watched schools of porpoises and corvally dash past the boat. Hungrily, Osun scoured the sky for gulls, wishing for their company and their noisy insane laughter.

By the end of the month, they would all be gone anyway, leaving Gull Island dead and naked until their return exactly the same time next year.

Times like these, he thought he understood the vast unnameable forces that kept the world on a pendulum; the mysterious precision of things; the forces that synchronised the rise and fall of moon and tide; the time that birds and fishes spawned and died and spawned again.

He had learned to understand the sea, to know its language. And that was not all. He was tied to it. Old Man Tigga who had chosen to go the way of the ocean, was his uncle after all. And in a way, his father had also gone like that. It was on the sea, in some dim place named Curacao that the mast of the white man's boat had broken and fallen across his back. The few years he lived afterwards was spent in bitterness and hatred at his crippled self.

And then of course there was their son. They were laughing at a private joke when the news was brought to them. Their laughter had died half way through. He had cried openly. But Lisa had only become dumb.

She hadn't taken it like other women. Had reserved the pain and tears for the darkness of their bedroom. The child was just eleven when he had drowned on the beach. The way she carried her grief frightened him, with the same simmering intensity, the same silent agony with which she had brought the boy into the world. Small as Lisa was, she bore pain as very few people could. That had made her different.

Childbirth and virginity the loss of which had meant so much to her were the moments in their lives when expression was purest. Each time she'd bled with love.

Osun stared at his hands, puzzled that he should be wanting to think of her now. After all these years. After everything.

ooooooo

The humming of the king line woke him. He must have fallen asleep, his back against the bow. He had brought the sail down and secured the tiller at an angle so that while he dozed the boat would move around in a tight circle. The mast of the craft was describing crazy arcs above his head and *Deliverance*, in the grip of some gigantic force was rocking like a leaf on the water. The king line was spooling out so fast, the heat from the friction against the wood raised the scent of burning pine.

Osun pulled himself to his feet, noting vaguely that the sun had already gone down and the sky was beginning to assume the grey impersonality of night. There was nothing to do but hold his breath and wait for the sudden, shuddering check of the line as it reached its end.

A fish. A giant. Everything told him that. And when the line finally came to a jarring, explosive halt, throwing him flat on his back, Osun realised what a monster it must be.

Whatever it was, it was running. It was running and *Deliverance* was at its mercy.

Bracing himself against the mast, he crouched low and waited for what he knew was about to come. The creature began to rise. Fast. From below.

This, he told himself, in a flush of exultation, was one of the moments for which he had been saving all his strength. He was worried though - that his own body might betray him. But it was worth the risk, even if it killed him. For he could imagine no greater glory than returning home, cured of his curse and with something the size of this monster whose awesome power was stretching the line that held it now, to the point of breaking. Already he could see the crowds on the beach, hear the voices, feel the eyes on him, the hands warm against his skin, congratulatory. He braced himself.

The ocean quaked.

A sudden swirl of water; the bare glimpse of a dark body. A monstrous mass of fin and flesh. A black back curving casually downwards. And then the gigantic flourish of tail-fins just above the water, a movement so incidental it seemed to contradict the enormity of the gesture. And its consequences. For it had just created a storm that almost swamped the boat, and with the same unthinking, stripped half of Deliverance's spine away, taking with it, the hook, the line and the anchor.

And then, well, it was gone. As simply as that. Gone. Leaving him staring at the sameness of a sea that belied the magnitude of what had taken place a few seconds ago.

Morning rose over dark water. The sun hung like a bruised eye above the eastern edge of the sea. He had arrived. He knew that by the nature of the water. It was opaque in a way that no sky could be reflected there. Even the movement of the boat was different. The sea tossed uncomfortably, like a sleeper trapped in dreams. And between moments of absolute stillness, the wind came in fitful bursts and spun the craft around. It was like that all the way till afternoon.

He waited, at one point lifting careless eyes at three birds that appeared from nowhere, a peculiarly joyous presence in the grey above. Yellow bills, perhaps; or white tails with their beautiful, bright streamers trailing behind. Not terns for sure, or pelicans. They did not fly that beautifully. His heart leapt. They had turned, all three of them, in a slow dark circle high above his head and then just hung there motionless on wings. Sky boats - flying frigates! Of all the creatures in the world, this was the one he would have most dearly wished to be. Osun watched them slip away spectre-like on the wind.

Lisa...

His thoughts returned to the fish. What was it? What could that have been? Now that he had partially recovered, his mind tried to span the dim reaches of the water below. Perhaps a tuna - he had seen how large they could become - over fourteen feet and several thousand pounds. Or perhaps a marlin. But a marlin would not respond like that. From the moment he struck, it would have risen and hit the air in a fury of tail and fin and spray. It would simply be a matter of time before it tired and still gasping with excitement, he would send the harpoon, unerring, deep through bone and flesh, into the small brain. Tunas were simpler, they ran until they drowned.

He could close his eyes and name a fish by the way it felt on the line. Osun was sure that he had not met anything like this creature before. This - whatever it was - was a silent and sinister intelligence all the more frightening because he never got to see it. That fish, he concluded, hadn't escaped him. It was he who had been saved.

He wondered whether Skido would believe him if he ever told him about the fish. It did not matter. Osun felt at ease. Secure. Being lost out here wasn't all that bad. Not bad at all. Not like when Lisa left him. That was the day after he struck her.

With one blow he'd killed everything that had been precious between them, his hand rising and exploding against her face and her eyes wide and unbelieving, more unbelieving than hurt because it seemed so senseless, so uncalled for. And he'd stood there watching the love drain out of her eyes and die. Even now, he did not understand exactly why he'd done it.

Perhaps it was the death of the child. Or his guilt. For even if he had not been there when the boy was lifted limp out of the water and laid out on the sand he believed he had something to do with it. The child had been holding his secret, hadn't he? An act of confidence for which he had been forever grateful to the boy and which he thought, had brought them even closer. It was not something he could admit to openly. Not in front of others. Even if he'd done it out of a reckless surge of pride to awe Jonah. He'd struck a dolphin; had gone against his own instincts and the knowledge instilled in every child long before they'd learned to bait a hook: that no-one ever struck a dolphin. A person looked into their eyes and knew exactly why. Dolphins did not speak, but they could respond to everything a soul was feeling.

It was no more than an impulse in the presence of his son, a reflex as old as time and blood and as natural as the stirrings in the groin. That was how it started. The boy was eleven then and as perfect a swimmer as anyone had ever seen. Long-boned he was, lean and strong as a purple reed. He had taken him out a mile that Sunday to lift the fish-pots he had laid around the edges of Short Horn. A bright day, he remembered, bright like brand new hooks. So bright in fact he had to narrow his eyes down to slits to see anything in the distance. It was the boy who had spotted the cloud of gulls first, a black smudge just above the horizon.

It took them an hour to get there. By then the mass of migrating corvally that had attracted the flock of gulls had moved further out. It was one of the biggest schools he'd ever seen, creating its own little whirlpool beneath the frenzied feeding of the gulls.

It was not as if he'd travelled the distance for any particular reason. In fact, even if he'd wanted to, he could not do anything but stand with his hand on the boy's shoulder and gape. He had not carried a net of any sort and the small line in the hold under the bow was useless without bait. There was the harpoon, of course, but using it would have been like using a cannon to shoot at mosquitoes. Again, it was the boy who noticed the turmoil in the middle of the moving mass of fish. Osun had to squint hard before he could spot them and when he did it was just the purple backs barely breaking surface, diving and rising in slick succession as they rounded up the fish.

It must have been the sudden pulse of curiosity and the oddity of that white body amongst the others which shifted his hand from the boy's shoulder and turned it towards the harpoon, so that when the dolphins rose and hit the air in that magical, curving chain that was both dance and exultation, his arm was already drawn full back. They had swum close enough for him to see the sheen of the sun on their skins and that curious ridge that ran along their mouths and made them seem to be perpetually smiling.

The white had disengaged herself in what must have been a display just for him and Jonah. With a twist of the powerful tail the creature scooped the water from the surface of the sea and fanned it out on the air in a spray so fine, it created rainbows in the sun.

He might have paid attention to the shrilling of the child but he thought it was just his excitement. On the fifth rising, the harpoon perfectly poised, Osun struck.

That cry!

Lord have mercy!

Didn't know to this day whether it was the dolphin or the boy. He'd turned around and found him crouched low in the boat, his hands grasping his sides as if it was he that had been wounded. Wounded, yes, because the dolphin had not died. And what happened afterwards, well, Jonah was there to prove that he had seen it: its companions did not leave that strangely pale and glistening creature there. They bore it away.

Osun couldn't tell how long he stood there with the boy staring at the slow procession till the waves and distance hid them.

Those eyes! Lord have Mercy, those red eyes. The creature had come close enough for him to look into them. He would never be able to forget those eyes.

It was those eyes he was remembering when almost exactly one year later, he knelt on the sand and eased the wet head of his son off the piece of tarpaulin.

Lisa had decided to leave him the very day that he confessed about the dolphin, and unable to bear the betrayal in her eyes, he'd turned around and struck her.

Osun rested his eyes on the water and covered his face.

He waited under a stiffening sky. The piece of tarpaulin he dug out of the tiny hold took the brunt of the rain when the sky eventually opened up. There was much more on the way. He could smell the coming storm. The air was tight and tense and crackling with the threat of it. And *Deliverance* was tired. He hoped that she could take it.

Osun drank the last of his water, ate some dried fish and threw the rest away. Without water, the salted fish would only worsen his thirst. Food was not a worry. He could manage. Anyway, the dolphin should be coming soon.

It was with idle eyes that he watched the boat approaching through the rain. At first he thought it was the white crest of a large wave. Then *Deliverance* rose on a swell and he saw it. A yacht, sails trimmed, dipping and rising. Coming his way. They'd seen him. It came close, gleaming white. White faces, staring down at him. Suddenly he remembered an old stone church, a tall cross and banks upon banks of pews and he, a small boy, standing before a robed figure and statues, hundred of gleaming statues staring back at him. Osun buried his face between his knees.

Some time after, he opened his eyes and wondered if he had been dreaming. But he looked up and around him and saw it disappearing, a white bird through the mist of rain.

The air was dripping with the suspense of the storm. He waited with some expectancy because he was sure it had something to do with the dolphin and his being there. Night had returned by the time the sky opened up and when it did, it was as if the whole world had suddenly come tearing down on him. The images returned, stiffly robed and polished. Osun called them by their names; then he prayed to them like his mother had taught him once, cursed them and prayed to them again. Then he tried to fight them off.

Deliverance, defiant of the wind, the rain, the thunder and the tide fought back like a thing possessed. Sometimes he sensed her falling, falling endlessly downwards. Osun died many times, each dizzying fall a new death. Tensely, he waited for the great engulfing wall of water. It never came. The craft recovered and brought him up again. It was on one of those upward surges that he was sure he heard his name, somebody calling:

Osunyin. Osunyin... Osunyin, Osunyin.

His first name. In full. Like his mother used to call him. Like Lisa always did.

Osunyin Osunyin... Osunyin Osunyin - a quick succession of breakers dying on a dark reef.

'Lisa?' He called back.

Morning. Osun slept through most of the day like a newly delivered child. When he opened his eyes, the sun was a bright brass coin burning his skin. He heard gulls before he saw them. He'd woken up to a strange peace, a peace that was reflected by the calmness of the water on which *Deliverance* now floated. Osun felt timid. This thing inside of him now was new and delicate. He felt afraid to move lest he should lose it.

How long had he been out here? Three days? Four? It felt like all his life. And he hadn't eaten. Wasn't hungry. Just tired - tired like *Deliverance* and, like her, at ease. Nothing moved him now, not even Gull Island when it rose up out of the sea before him. It occurred vaguely to him that they had come full circle. The storm had driven him back. He had accepted the fact without question, more concerned now with guiding the craft towards the windward side of the island.

The beach curved like a wide grin before him, piled high with shells, mangled bits of clothing, and lengths of wood that were bleached bone-white by the sun and air. He remembered the yacht and wondered if they had made it to the mainland; decided that they couldn't have. Like him, they had been too far away from anywhere to have escaped the storm.

At the last moment Osun changed tack and guided *Deliverance* into the stony leeward harbour. Much quieter there, at least. But it was more in obedience to an old feeling - the one that he could hardly put his finger on although he recognised it instantly - that he had suddenly changed direction. Truth was, the feeling had been there a long time - just after Lisa - not painful but persistent, like a grain of sand inside a shoe. The feeling grew and translated itself into a strangely sexual stirring.

Osun sat in the boat until the sun became a bit of burning coal on the very edges of the ocean. The sky smouldered above him with a quiet rage. To die - and to die like that - was beautiful. Quietly, leaving all that beauty behind. For a while he sat there undecided, eyes fixed gratefully on the boat. *Deliverance* had been good to him.

Stiffly, he clambered over the side of the craft. The world spun. He was much weaker than he'd realised. The foot. He hadn't thought of the foot. Wasn't hurting anymore. Couldn't remember if it ever did these past few days out here. He climbed carefully up the stone beach and chose one of the great flat boulders there. He wanted to rest. Just a while. Sleep the sleep he hadn't slept for so many months now. Since he'd taken Lisa away. The stone was warm with the heat it had absorbed during the day; warm with the warmth of life, it felt like.

Chest bared to the sky, Osun followed its domed curve with his eyes. Another realisation, another certainty as he thought of the horizon that had circled him these past days. Everything in life was circles. Everything important: earth and moon and stars; his head, his heart, life itself. And it was not by chance that the mouth itself, once opened to make meaning of the world, became an 'O' of sorts. God expressed god's self in circles. Osun stared up at the world, astounded.

Some way off, the water was a multitude of murmurings, like a congregation deep in prayer. The stones, stretched out on either side of him were giant pews. For a moment the white images appeared and made him smile. There was a soft humming in his head that drowned the psalming of the sea below. The boats from the shore that he'd escaped were coming and he was travelling away from them. Fast, exultant because he was certain they could not catch him. Not now or ever. The Gate was before him, foaming high.

The waves, raising hell above him, were obliging him at last. They froze, and there below he saw it all, exactly as it had been brought to him in dreams. Except the whiteness. Stupid of him to think it was the dolphin. Lisa had been wearing white that last time. In white, that was how he'd dressed her before he'd brought her out here and rested her. After he'd struck her again, struggling with himself to stop. But his hand would not allow him. Was better that way; not so? Couldn' bear to see her leave. Had to make 'er stay, not so? Else, he would have lost his mind.

Smiling, Osun reached out beneath the waves, touched the whiteness and was covered.

Night came and settled over the island. A fish, in what might have been a momentous, life-saving dash, momentarily broke the surface and struck air before being reclaimed by the living water.

A soft wind rocked the boat, cheeked the loose sail out and swung the bow of the craft towards the open sea. It hung there tentatively; bobbing gently; battered now, but still very much alert with something of the spirit of the man who had so painstakingly created her. A firmer, harder wind took hold of her and glided *Deliverance* out towards the open water.

A gull laughed softly in the darkness and was silent.

Ku-Kus:
De Laughin Tree

Granny didn have no problem when the white man tell she that she stupid. She didn give im back no forward answer. She didn even cuss im afterwards behind he back an call im no sand fly, no beke, no big guts, half bake so-and-so from Englan. No redarse, no lobsterface, no bleachout nothing. And I tell meself it wasn fair cos if was me dat even raise mih eyelash too fast at she, she would ha grab de palette by de door an all now so I would ha been rubbing mih skin an bawling.

I tell meself dat mebbe she tired becos this quarrel with Missa Coleridge start off long time. Long before my mother leave me with she an say how she goin to Trinidad to make a livin and she goin send money and after a little time she goin send for me. I still waitin, like I still waitin for my Granny to put some words in Missa Coleridge tail. Nobody never talk to my Granny like dat an get away just so. People always comin an askin if we want to buy someting: provision, fish, sweetie, even costlymetics from de Avon lady (Granny does always ask de lady where she does want her to put dem tings she sellin) and once a man come offerin to sell a little donkey and Granny ask him rough what he want she to do with a little jackass, ain't he think it have nuff Jackass round here arready? De man look at she an ask she if she talkin bout sheself an I sure he still regret it becos she tell im a coupla tings dat make im look like if he wish he never born far less to step inside my Granny yard an ask she if she want to buy donkey.

Now I never fraid nobody. An I had three mind to put some serious wud in Missa Coleridge tail meself, specially when my Granny wasn goin to do it! People always tellin de Ole Lady how I rude but if is one time I feel glad for mih rudeness was when dat white man come an tell my granmother how she stupid. Ah tell yuh I feel it; I feel it in mih bones. BIG PEOPLE does get away with too much freshness, jus' because dey feel dey BIG. In fact if it wasn for Granny palette, and de fact dat BIG PEOPLE does go an tell she all de tings I does say back to dem, it have lot o time I does feel to put some serious wuds in BIG PEOPLE tail, specially when dem aggravate me and tell me dat I got too much mouth. I does want to ask dem if dem have myopia, if dem arthritis reach up in dem eye; if dem don't have no acquaintanship wit measurement; if dem cyah see dat is a little mouth I have. Cos I like to put wuds. I like to learn an practise wuds especially for people who talk to me as if I is dey child, as if I don't have no mother just because she gone away an never send for me. In fact sometimes when Granny vexin over my mother never writing an sayin, 'dog I reach, or dog how is de chile getting on', I does put some wuds to my mother, only in my head though, cos Granny wouldn like it.

Is de same way I feel when Missa Coleridge come and order my Granny to sell she place to he. I 'member de first time he come he was grinnin all over he face. He tell she how everybody done sell out deir little piece over de sea, as if she didn notice, and seein dat all she friends gone to a nicer place down by de Chichiree near de swamp, didn she think dat was a good idea to go an live wid dem?

Granny kinda smile an tell im, no she didn think so. I see how red and upset Missa Coleridge get. Although all of im was red arready, he get even redder. I don't think he was expectin it, specially since everybody sell deir land to im without a peep, an move down by de swamp as soon as he ask dem. I watch at im get red like cook crayfish an it mind me o de time when Missa Prissy wid the nice big car an pretty pants an shirt uses to come to Leena house an stay dere whole weekend. Den he stop an start to go to Miss Marcelle house becos she did jus come back from Canada. I member how Miss Leena uses to look at Marcelle, specially when she getting out o Missa Prissy car. Missa Coleridge look like dat when Granny tell im, no. And he didn say nothing more. He just pull off he white canvas hat an start to fan he face real fast. An den he walk off.

Now de same way I does look at a sky an know when rain makin up to fall, I know was trouble coming from de way dat man walk off an jump inside he car. Granny know dat too cos even if she didn batten up de window an look up at de roof to make sure dem hole up deh plug tight an proper, she mouth gone tight and she eye turn flat an dark, as if all de battening happenin inside o she.

'Ku-Kus,' she say (is how she does call me an I not suppose to tell nobody why) 'Ku-Kus go bring de grip come gimme!'

I go.

'Put it on de floor,' she say.

I put it.

'Open it,' she say.

I try. 'I can't open it Granny. It tight.'

'Rudeness is all you good for,' she say in a kind o frettin way, only dat she wasn frettin. Sometimes I notice how she hand does tremble. Is what I does call ole people tremble.

Sometimes I does practise to tremble like dat. But hers is better dan mine cos hers is a natral you cant do nothing about it tremble. Dis tremble dat she hand tremble now was a little different still. Was a shakin dat start from she shoulder and sort of work itself all de way down to she finger. Dat worry me. Cos old as she is, she not de kinda o pusson you kin make tremble easy. A pusson try to come at she and she kin hold dem back with a look o with a laugh. Most times just a coupla wuds does do.

She kind o straighten up as much as she back allow she and she look at me same way she did look at me dat evenin I was sittin down on de step an puttin some wuds to me mother in mih mind.

She watch at me an say, 'Feather,' (dat's another name she does call me an I not goin to tell nobody why). 'Feather,' she say, 'Don't ferget about yuh mother, jus because she ferget about we. But yuh have to tell yerself dat she never goin write we an she never goin send for you.'

Was sad I feel, not for meself but for Granny. An same time I put some wuds to meself an say, 'Ku-Kus Granny damn right to bring dat palette to y'arse sometimes, even when you think you don't deserve it, cos you does ferget how hard she try with you. Ent she does send you to school? Ent she does give you a piece o meat same size as she when she cook an sharin food? Ent she does sew up dem hole in yuh clothes, even if she finger tremblin an she could hardly see? Ent? Ku-Kus you does ferget is we alone on a little hill, in a little house, in front o de sea. An dat little house only stay stand up because Granny decide dat it wont fall down s'long as we live in it. So why you does give er so much trouble, what more you want? EH?'

I was puttin dem wuds to meself while Granny was lookin at me in dat serious kind o way. Same time de grip open an it leggo de nicest smell I ever smell. Ain't got no nicer smell in de world dan cinnamon an sandalwood an camphor and a whole heap of ole time smell mix up. Dat's how granny grip did smell.

When de grip open she look at me again an say, real serious, 'Feather, it have a lot o different way to fight. When I had strength in mih body, I was strong as any man. Ask yuh granfadder who try to hit me once. He could never use dat hand de same way after. Trouble was I had to do all de hard work to cure an mek it better. Ask im.'

She does tell me a lot o tings to ask or tell my granfadder. Trouble was he done gone an dead long before I born. An I member de first time she ask me to ask im something. I take she serious and start looking about de house, even under de bed to see if he was hidin there o something. Dat was de first time I make she laugh so much, 'Chile how you chupid so?' An yunno, was funny how good dat question make me feel cos was same like when she bring me behin de house to bathe me proper an she hand was rough an gentle at de same time. Not like when Missa Coleridge come in we yard an tell we how we stupid.

'Open dis,' Granny say. She hand me a yellow piece o paper dat fold up small like if nobody was never intend to open it. It smell o all dem nice tings in de grip. An when I open it, it had a drawin on de left hand side on top, an a pretty piece of string dat stick to a red round ting on de paper, like a big drop o blood dat mix up with candle wax an harden. I get a little bit 'fraid of it becos I never see a piece o paper dat look so serious. If paper was priest then this would ha be de Pope. Not even de big leather Bible dat Granny had did look so serious to me.

'What dat is?' I ask she.

'Read it,' she tell me. Now Teacher always tell me how I is a boss reader, an is mosly because I interested in puttin wuds to people who fret me up dat I does be always readin. I learn quick. Dat is de only way dat I could answer back BIG PEOPLE an don't get a taste o Granny palette for mih rudeness. Like when Missa JoJo shout at me for bathin naked below de standpipe by de road an call me a shameless little soanso. Dese is de wuds I put to im. 'Nutting obnoxious o anonymous, o even obstreperous about havin de benediction of water on meself Missa JoJo, Sah.' An I went on bathin, like if he wasn dere.

He sort of shut down one eye an open he mouth an try to tell me someting more, but he find dat he didn have no tongue to give me back high quality, bigtime wuds like me. I smile to meself because I did even put de benediction in deliberate just in case he tell Granny, because was a word dat Pastor does use all de time in church an everybody know dat it mean niceness o someting close to dat. So yuh see I not easy puttin wuds.

But! Dat paper was different. It write like how Moses in de Bible would ha write if he did like to put wuds. I always tell myself dat dem longtime Biblepeople was too ignorant. Dem didn know how to cuss. An is many a time I wish I was livin in dem days to teach Missa Moses or Missa Joshua or Missa Job or Missa Soloman a coupla tings 'bout using wuds. All now so me too woulda been a Book in de Bible an people might ha been readin De Wuds accordin to Ku-Kus, Chapter soanso, Verse soanso..

Anyway I start to read:

In the name of God Amen.

I, John Munchford, in the Parish of St. Albans on the 30th day of October 1904, Anno Domini, being weak of body but of sound and perfect disposing mind and memory praised be God, bequeath unto Ursula Auguste Jameson, a plot of land measuring half a hectare squared, the which begins at Hill Cray Rise and proceeds northwards towards the adjoining estate of Carl Strong, said land having no agricultural merit and ceded by myself in lieu of and in recognition of

*thirty years service as maid servant in the
employment of the Munchford household.*

*It is also hereby deemed that the Inheritor of the
aforementioned property becomes henceforth sole
proprietor of said and shall have the powers vested
in herself by law to bequeath or dispose of said
property as she deems fit.*

John Munchford.

When I done read, I look at Granny an say. 'And den it
have some big time scrawl, like if somebody wrap up a piece
o wire, drop it in a bottla ink an den press it on de paper.'

'What it say?'

'Is a signicha,' I answer. 'It not s'pose to say nutting.' Same
time I tell meself dat I must practise to write me name just
like dat.

'Nuh. De paper what it say?'

'I jus done read it for you,' I tell she. An I start scratchin
mih ears which I does always do when I little bit embarrass
cos I could see dat Granny wasn satisfy at-all, at-all. An I
wasn neider. I damn vex dat people could be so bold face as
to write down a whole heap o wuds on serious paper an I
couldn understand it. As if dem want to make a fool o me in
front o my granmother.

'It say someting bout land,' I tell she soon as I ketch mih
breath, 'land an property. It look like if it say so.'

I figure dat for she to have serious lookin paper like dis in
she grip with pretty cord and candle wax dat mix wid blood
dat mention land an property well... I figure it have to say
someting serious and it could only be dat she own de place.
Besides nobody didn have no doubt dat was she place till
Missa Coleridge come an say she have to sell, an ask she iffen
she really own it.

'I sure it say so, Granny. We definitely own dis property
an land - perhaps.'

Now de time dat man tell Granny dat she stupid wasn de first time he come. I member de first time he come how nice he was. He was even smilin. Wasn a pretty smile, I notice de yellow teeth an how dem thin little lips sort o pull back over dem, but he speak polite and proper. He touch de brim o de white sailor cap he wearin an say, 'Evening Maam,' an Granny say, 'Evenin Suh.' He say, 'How're you today?' Granny say, 'I awright think you. De little ramatism does bother me sometimes but I survivin by de grace o de Almighty.'

De man smile an brush he shortsleeve white shirt. An I vex becos I feel dat Granny coulda find some prettier wuds to answer with. Cos wuds is dere to use an it have a lotta dem, she coulda tell he dat she not complacent an she aint got no botheration, dat she was of salubrious constitution an feelin dam well good with it. But no, she tell im bout she ramatism!

'Nothing grows here, I see,' de man say. He look round bout he an smile. 'Not good for gardening, is it?'

An yunno, someting funny happen when he say dat; I look round me an was like if it was de first time I see de place we live in; dat de only ting dat grow, in truth, was mint grass dat was brown an parch like asham, and a whole heap o cochineel dat nobody could use for nothing except to wash deir hair. I see dat de hill dat all o we was livin on was dry an white like flour. All everybody had was dryness an some dead mint grass an cactus. I notice dat we was plant between de big wide sea in front an de Chichiree swamp behind, an de only ting dat conneck we with de outside world was one little dust road dat go right down to de pretty pink beach below.

'Is de will o de Lord,' Granny answer. Dat fret me but I didn say nutting.

Missa Coleridge didn smile dis time. He jus walk back to he car.

Next time he come he look a lot more serious. By dat time everybody know dat he want to buy up de place an everybody was preparing to sell real quick cos was a lot o money he was payin.

He offer Granny money an she tell im, no, De Lord was takin care of her well enough think yuh. Missa Coleridge look at she as if she mad. Dem turkey wrinkle dat hang down below he neck get kind o purple and even more wrinkleup, an he han was very agitate. He look at she an den he look at me, cos I was in de yard sort o pretendin dat I was sweepin, den he look at she again, den he look round im an say, 'D'you expect me to accept that? Everybody's sold up. They were glad to have the money. Your government even undertook to move their house for them free! What reason have you got for not moving with your people?'

Granny didn answer. I look at de man under me eye and it occur to me he had a point. Since he change de way dat place look for me I didn like it dere no more. All my friends done move. Dem mother and fadder had money dat Missa Coleridge give dem. Some o dem was even buildin concrete house. So how come Granny gettin on so foolish?

'Maybe the child has something to say about this?'

Now ever since dat man start comin he never say nothin to me; he never even see me. Now he want me to say someting an make contrary wit my Granny.

I look up quick. De man smile at me. I look at Granny. She didn look as if she was payin me no mind. In fact, I feel as if she was encouragin me. So I put down de broom an I wipe mih mouth an dis is what I say: I say, 'Granny doesn got de dispositioning to concur nobody proposition.' De man look at me as if I hit im. Wuds, I tell you! Dem ting is wundaful! I thought de man was goin to fall. But he push up he chest an say, he say, 'My Gaad!'

Well dat make im leave de yard very quick and I thought to meself dat dem wuds o mine goin make us see de last of im. But a coupla weeks after, he come back and call my Granny stupid. And like I say arready, something inside me tell me dat it wasn goin to end up easy. I could see dat Granny know dat too becos dat same night after she put back de serious paper, she didn sleep at all. Or if she sleep it was like dem boat I use to watch fightin to cross de bad water near Goat Point dere. In all my time wid she, my Granny never toss and groan so.

Dat night I wonder bout everyting. What my mother was doin in Trinidad? Mebbe she had a husban now and I had brothers an sisters I didn know? Mebbe she did never like me and she did decide from de start dat she wasn goin send for me. Granny tell me dat my mother was still a girl when she went somewhey an 'pick me up'. An I member askin Granny why mih mother didn put me back down, or jus leave me where I was, iffen she didn want me, cos I sure by now dat I would ha been livin wit a rich mother an fadder who'd a pick me up an want me for deir chile. Dat mek she laugh. She tell me she wish life was easy like dat. An besides if it did happen dat way, she wouldn ha been my Granmother.

Granny get quiet close to mornin. An I suppose she must ha fall asleep. But not me. All dat thinkin wouldn leave me alone. An when I get tired thinkin, I find meself lissenin to, well, de worl. De night was like a pusson out dere rubbin himself agains de house. I could hear de sea too, like a million ole woman quarrelin mongst demself. Even de wind dat pass across de galvanise. Ghosts, I thought, a gadderin of ghosts dat makin church above we head and de noise I hearin was de shufflin o dem foot. But it didn' frighten me, cos I had Granny close, and nothing never frighten me when me an Granny lay down close.

Before I fall asleep to sort o keep she company, I member de las ting dat she say to me when dat white man left.

'Feather,' she say. 'Is tired dese ole bone tired, chile. Dem see too much in dis life arready. All dem wan to do is rest.'

'Feather,' she say. I didn answer but I lissen. 'You tink dis lan useless for true?'

She always tell me dat I mus never lie for she an if I have
to lie it must be only to protect meself, but I mus never lie for
she. So I didn lie. 'Yes, Granny,' I say.

'Why?' She say.

'Cos everybody sell dem own an gone to live cross by de
swamp, an Merle fadder goin to buy a Lan Rover an Joan say
she mother goin sen she to Englan to study history when she
get big; an Jean say she gettin a big big dolly for Chrismas
and she goin travel round de islan an write everyting down
dat people say, an Jacob say is only we dat stupid an'

'Ku-Kus?'

'Uh?'

'You say teacher say you bright?'

'Yes Granny cos I know big wuds.'

'Well answer dis: if dis property so wutless how come de
Mister want it so bad, an nobody didn know it wutless till he
start to tell dem so?'

Yunno, I never thought o dat! Dat never cross mih mind.
Yunno, dis Granny o mine!

'Ku-Kus?'

'Gran?'

'S'pose I say dat it have a whole heap o tings big wuds
can't teach you.'

'It don't. What about dat paper? Is dat paper dat make
Missa Coleridge cant touch we; an is dem big wuds self dat
make it so.'

'Is not de big wuds is what de big wuds mean. All it mean
is dat dis piece o land belong to me fair an proper. An look
how easy dat is to say. De people who write dat paper jus too
dam show off an pretenshus.' An she laugh kinda dry an funny
an I didn like dat laugh at all, specially becos she was lookin
at me as if she wasn talkin bout no paper. Den she face get
serious. 'I hardly got de time to see de endin o dis fight. Is ole
yuh Granny gettin ole.'

I tell she dat I know how to fight and if was stone she

want me to stone dat man, next time he come is stone I glad to stone im.

'Nuh,' she say. 'If yuh stone im den we lose. With people like dat is a different kind o fight yer have to fight. Not like we does fight an not like dem does fight.'

'How den?'

'You mix dem up, Feather. You mix dem up an make a different way.'

'I don unnerstan.'

'Patience, chile.'

An yunno, is a long, long time after dat I realise dat she did give me de answer right deh.

Is when Missa Coleridge come back de next time and she ask me to show im de paper but don let im touch it dat tings really turn sour. Granny tell me long time afterwards when tings was comin to a end dat nutting in Missa Coleridge worl make him prepare for people like we to refuse him anyting. It have people who tink dat dem own everyting, like if dem entitle to it long before dem even born. Dat dem teach deir chilren to believe someting is deirs even before dem know what ownin mean. Dat for people like we to tell dem no, is worse dan steppin on dem big toe o spittin in dem eye. Is a belief dat dem born inside of - same way dat a fish o tadpole does born surround by water.

Mebbe dat was why Missa Coleridge get on like dat when I point de paper in he face an show im de stamp o de candleblood.

De man blow like a lambi shell, tellin we how we silly; how we is ignoramus (I write dat down), how Granny cantankerous (I write dat down too) how everybody move and we ignorant not to accept de money an move too, how we obstructin progress; how de govment give im rights an we hambuggin dem rights; how he wish de little chicken coop of a house fall down on we an kill we (yes he say dat!); an how it ain got nobody who goin help we when we dead, jus wait

101

an see. An if we tink dat we goin spoil he plans, we go soanso see!

I get so vex I nearly put some wuds to he, but I member what Granny tell me bout big wuds an little meanin, an even if I didn agree wid she, it sort o throw cold water on mih tongue, so I constraint mihself. An I have to say, I did find it flippin flabbergastin.

Nex day Granny send me an call Missa JoJo.

'Joseph,' she say. 'I want you to get me a laughin tree.'

Missa JoJo laugh. But me, I wasn laughin becos I hear bout all kinda tings dat tree does do: dem does sway in de wind, an whisper in de breezes, an sigh an groan an even fall down in hurricane, but I never hear bout no tree dat does laugh. Missa JoJo laugh again an tell she, yes.

An when he leave, Granny rub she chin an say to me dat she sorry she insult de man who try to sell she de little donkey, dat she shoudda buy de creature becos she goin be needin a lotta manure!

ooooooo

I didn know what I did expect Missa JoJo to bring for Granny but it definitely wasn what he pull out from hi jola bag an pass over to she so secret secret. A stick. A little piece o nothing. I was well disappoint and I make sure I show it. To mek tings worse, Granny walk round de house and den de boundary o de land for a whole day before she jook it in de ground an leave it dere. Den she have de face to call me an tell me dat is my responsibility. I have to water it an manure it, an whatever happen to she afterwards, I mus never root it up an never let nobody touch it. An even if she dead an gone she goin be watchin me to make sure I care dat stick. I don tink I ever see my Granny look so serious before.

A lotta tings begin to happen straight afterwards. Dat question dat Granny ask me bout why Coleridge want de lan so bad sort o answer itself for me. First ting, a whole heap o truck arrive with sand an gravel an drums o tar. An den a bulldozer wit caterpillar wheel come. After dat a stone leveller arrive to keep it company an mek a whole heap of noise in people head.

An yunno! De same people who uses to be we friends, who Coleridge send off to live in de swamp; dem same people come out with shovel an tray an start widenin de dust road an pouring tar an gravel, an cookin, an eatin lunch by de road. An soon de road wasn a dust road no more.

Dat Missa Coleridge used to stan up in de selfsame road mongst all dem people an point he quailup, red finger at my granmother an say tings, an dem people who used to be we friend, who we used to borrow a pinch o we salt, an a cup o we sugar, dem selfsame people used to laugh with im.

Mornins after waterin de tree I goin to school wit me little hanbag an mih lunch in me Dano pan and dem lookin at me an shooshooin mongst demself an laughin.

Joan fadder always askin me how is de ole lady; but I never answer he cos he have a kinda grin in he eye which I didn like at all. But I have to say de road was easier to walk on an it was pretty an shiny like a ribbon you buy in de shop an iron it till it smooth an shiny.

I feel foolish wit me Dano pan o lunch cos everybody mother buy dem three an fourstorey foodcarrier to bring deir lunch to school in. An it wasn no steam fig an breadfruit without no meat eider, cos dem mother an fadder wuckin for Missa Coleridge and dem have payday every week. So imagine de vex I vex when I reach home an Granny siddown dere an say she not sellin no land to nobody.

After de road, more truck come with cement an lumber an all sort o ting. For a whole year de worl start changin before me eye jus so.

Dat hotel tek five years to build. I count dem. Granny count dem too. A lotta pretty concrete house, brown an white wit a swimmin pool, dat was bright in de sun like a white man eye, shoot up over de sea.

'Cottages,' Jacob fadder say. 'Cottages wit lectric light an runnin water, an bath an everyting. Is progress. Yuh can't beat white man for brains.'

It was plain to see, so I couldn find no wuds for dat. But Granny had a few.

'Ask im if he allow to go an bathe dere or get a bucket o water in Coleridge pipe to drink. Ask im if all de work he work for Coleridge itten dat mek him have electric too.'

So I ask im. An he get vex an call me a rudemout soanso who didn have no mother, an a ole shegoat for a Granmother who de hell I tink I is!

I cry.

I didn tell Granny. Cos it hit me dat it didn have nothing dat she could do an even if it hurt me, was true what Jacob fadder say.

But Missa JoJo must ha tell she, becos dat night she was extra nice to me. She fry plantain and give me, seein as I like fry plantain so much. An she call me, 'Darlin.' Now, when Granny call me darlin is like she givin me someting nicer dan a sweetie. Is a wud dat don come from she mouth so easy.

'Darlin,' she say, 'don let none o dem upset you. How much chilren it had in class today?' I was so fed up I didn wan to answer she. Was a question she always ask me ever since de trouble start an I could never figure out why. Sometimes she even ask de name o dem who didn come to school. Is how I come to tell she every time I reach home eggzackly who an who stay home an what an what day dem sick with cold o fever.

'Halfclass,' I mumble. She didn ask me no more question, p'raps becos she see dat I was hatin de place an I was not likin she no mo, an I didn want to walk de road to go to school. She was lookin at me kinda sorry. 'Ku-Kus,' she say, 'You notice how dem chilren sickin all de time?'

'Uh huh.'

'You notice how you never sick?' I coudda tell she dat it have sick an *sick* an I was sick of all de aggravitin from everybody. But she would ha say I rude.

'You not sickin cos you not livin by de swamp. Is all dat bad water an mosquito cross dere.'

I still didn say nothin.

'Feather? I wan to show you someting.' She was callin me in dat ole lady voice o hers. She didn use to have dat voice befo, but since Missa Coleridge start on we, I hearin a tired, tired voice dat frighten me cos was like a ole mango dat dry up in de sun. Like it was comin from another place inside o she.

Dese days de only time I see she happy was when she waterin dat tree. First coupla months dat piece o stick didn shift. I tell she dat it dead an she tell me no, it was jus gatherin it strength. But I could see it worry she, cos even in de middle o de night she uses to get up an tek de lamp to go an look at it. Mornin time she water it an feed it wit a little manure dat Missa JoJo bring for she. She even used to talk to it. An den one mornin I hear she crow - was de way she use to laugh - and when I run out I see she tremblin with excitableness.

'Look,' she say. 'It takin off. It takin off!'

I watch dat stick an I watch Granny, an I ask mihself, 'Ku-Kus wha you goin do, an who goin tek care o you till you get big an get a work cos yuh mother ain goin send for you an now yuh Granny jus gone dotish.'

But she was right though. Is de next week I see what she mean by takin off. Cos sudden so, dat piece o stick was full o leaf an in a coupla months you'd ha tink it been growin dere all de time.

So when she tell me she wan to show me someting I say mebbe was another coupla leaf dat tree sprout out an she wan to show me.

But no, she didn take me outside. She take me to de

window. Now, all de botheration mek me ferget to tell y'all dat Missa Coleridge was buildin a highrise someting right in front o we. It didn finish yet but it had four concrete pillar an a whole heap o iron dat push up to de sky. Jacob fadder say was a skyscraper an Joan fadder say he lie, is a big time water tank for dem tourist when we have Dry Season, cos even if dem touris not too fussy about bathin, dem does really suffer when dem thirsty.

Was all dat barring up dat people didn like too much. Coleridge start putting block around everyting. He build a tall wall round de hotel. He block up de road down to de beach. He bar off de best part of it for dem touris and den he start buildin dat skyscrapin water tank.

In truth nobody never get to know what it was for, cos Granny see to dat for good.

Was evenin and on top o de upset, I was frettin an fedup an fussup bout everyting, so I didn wan to watch no laughin tree dat didn laugh an count how much new leaf it have.

'Yes Gran,' I say, 'it growin.'

'Ferget de tree, chile. Jus watch cross dere by de side o where de sun is.'

So I lif up mih head a little bit. An yunno, I custom to seein de side o where de sun an de sea an de sky is, mosly from de corner o me eye. I custom to seein all o dat when I doin someting else. I didn see nothing special in dat. Was not like playin cricket o rounders, o practising big wuds. De sea was de sea an de sun was de sun an dat was dat. Is so I always use to tink till Granny make me stop an watch what happen to de world come evenin time.

Now people know dat I is a pusson dat know wuds. When come to wuds I full of expertise. But I tell y'all dis right now: it ain got no wuds in no book dat could tell you what happen cross dat sea water when de sun goin down. It ain got no dream in de world dat could dream dem light an colour.

You watch dat sea turn wine, turn blood, turn fire an smoke

an you feel little an big, an sure 'bout everyting same time dat you thinkin dat you dunno where you goin, o who you is, o why you is what you is in de first case.

Like it had a voice inside o me dat was sleepin all de time an is only dat sight dat wake it up. An it tell me dat nutting can't belong to nobody. Dat dem fish down dere an Granny laughin tree got de same flippin rights as you an me an Missa Coleridge. It make you dont want to dead but same time you don feel fraid to dead no mo. An yunno, on top of everyting, it mek me glad dat I have Granny for mih granmother an jus sorry for mih mother. Was a funny kind o sorry too, soft an warm like a pillow you does sleep on.

'Praise de Lord,' Granny say, really soft so I nearly didn hear she. But I hear, an it make a lot o sense to me cos dis sky was bigger, prettier, brighter dan de nicest church window in de world. I was very sure o dat even if de onliest church window I ever see was de big Catlic one in St. George's.

Dat was when Granny look at me straight in mih eye an say, 'Dat, Ku-Kus is what Missa Coleridge wan to take from we. Is what he want for hisself an hi friends alone. Not even to let we have a little piece.'

We stay deh till night come up like smoke from down behin de sea an wipe out everyting. Dat mek me sad an want to cry. But Ganny rub mih head an tell me to dont ferget dat de same sun was comin back tomorrow. Dat was life, she say. After a while, life does take back de tings it put dere, specially when it get old, and it put back someting dat was de same but a lot fresher to replace it. Missa Coleridge was chupid she tell me, cos he was too blind to see dat. He behave as if de sky belong to im and he friends alone.

I think bout it a lot. We didn have no road no more to go down to de beach cos Coleridge block it off an make a pretty little set o steps dat go only from he swimmin pool straight down to de sand. And it had a big wall round everyting with a gate. An he pay Jacob fadder forty dollars every month to wear a blue shirt an khaki pants to prevent all o we from usin it. An he pay Joan fadder fifty dollars every month to wear a khaki shirt an khaki pants to prevent we from bathin on de part o de beach dat had nice pink sand cos dem touris complainin all de time dat we, de natives, comin too close to dem an dey don want us to tief deir tings. Even Jacob fadder an Joan fadder didn like dat name. Dat was why dey was strict with trespassers only when Missa Coleridge was around. Still, nobody complain cos dey fraid dat missa Coleridge goin stop dem sellin straw basket, an little steel pan, an coconut hat, an seashell, an all dem tings dat nobody didn have no use for, except touris.

'Is why you mus promise me Ku-Kus dat when I gone you never goin get rid o de property. An dat tree, treat it like you chile, treat it like I try my best to treat you, like you mother never treat you. Be good to de property an de tree.'

Now I tired ask she what so special bout dat tree an all she say is dat I askin too much question. De property. Dat was how she start to call it now. Before Missa Coleridge come it was jus 'de little piece o lan' or 'de groun behin de house', but now it get promote to property.

Dese days, too, she keep talkin bout when she gone as if she was goin somewhere. But is true I never see she so content specially when she watch dat laughin tree dat didn laugh at all.

And yunno, de funny ting was, Granny didn have to tell me to tek care o she property, becos dat voice dat wake up in me when I watch de sun go down, same voice tell me dat it ain got no way I goin pass Granny property to nobody, long as I live even if I have to make meself a legalisin lawyer o someting like dat to fight dem back.

oooooooo

Time pass an I get kind o proliferate wit wuds (yuh see what

Ah mean?). Is like when I was leaving school an Teacher ask me what I want to become. I coudda tell im I want to be like mih Granny (God bless she), which was true but I say I want to be a psychoepistemologist. He ask me what dat was an he look kinda suspicious like if I was cussin a bad word in de smart. I tell im to figure it out for hisself an I walk off.

Is de same ting I tell de govment people when I apply for de work in de post office and dem must ha figure dat if I could write an pronounce heavy wud like dat, it mean dat I could read bad hanwriting easy. So I get de work.

Was de same year dat Granny call me by me real name an close she eye for good. An wasn jus Granny alone. Dat fight between she an Missa Coleridge never stop. Over de years dat follow was like de whole govment come to we little yard to force we to move out. A man from de Ministry of Touris come an tell we how we mus give up de lan cos we standin in de way of evolution.

Granny uses to leave me to handle dem people so. I tell de fella dat evolution is a Darwin phenomenon dat have relevance an impertinence, an application to sheep an goat an bacterias so is want I did want to know iffen he is extenuatin dat we is some kind o ectoplasm o what.

Dat confuse he an he left straight away, upset. Den Public Works arrive in overalls an hard hat an I didn bother to put no heavy wuds to dem seein as dem is not s'pose to be eddicated like me. Besides I didn wan to throw no pulse to swine, so is straight bad wud I cuss dem, which I will desist myself from quotin here.

I tell Ministry of Education dat dem is irrelevant cos I soon to leave school anyway.

Foreign Affairs was a nice young girl dat run back to de road soon as she see me. I s'pose was becos she see me with Granny cutlass in mih hand cos I was cleanin dem weed round de laughin tree. But I stop she wit a few big wuds and den I cuss she up an down, an den back up again an dat was dat.

Agriculture nearly get me. I never see a fella nice so. Black an smooth an long like a gar fish, wid nice nice eye. He look at de tree, den he look at me an den he look at Granny and I sure a flash o someting pass between dem two. Was better dan a smile an faster dan lightning, but I know dat I did see it. Agriculture turn round, sort o thinkin, an look at Coleridge hotel below. An you know what he do? He flash dem pretty teeth at we. An even iffen I feel little selfconscientious to say so, dem moonlight teeth mek me feel same like when Granny show me de sky dat evenin long time back. Except de feelin was a little more localise.

'*Arbores Sinistres*, he say. 'It start to... er?'

'Happen soon,' Granny tell im a little bit too fast for me. But mih tongue was too block up for me to ask im what it was dat tree didn start to do yet.

Well a month after, I learn. It start with a cackle. One bright evenin I hear cacklin an I run out. Was Granny under de tree an she was holdin open she hand like if she was beggin it for someting and she was cacklin like mad.

'Come an see dat chile. It start laughin. Come an see dat Ku-Kus.' An she grab mih hand an hold it up same way like she hold up hers. Well was only a little bit o water drippin from dem leaf an branch. I tell she so, an how I dam well disappoint cos I didn see why she fussin over a little bit o dew.

She cackle again an tell me how I dunno how to use mih brain. 'What time o day it is, Ku-Kus?'

I look round me an tell she, 'Evenin.'

'Dew does fall in de evenin? An when last rain fall round here?'

Dat was when it hit me. Dat tree was drippin water in de middle o Dry Season. How come? I wan to know. But, 'Now I could rest in peace,' was all she say.

Well God grant she satisfaction to see de first part: how Coleridge big white wall jus begin to split apart startin with a little crack an den growin, growin, growin till was like a mouth dat somebody bust open with a cuff. It happen over four months an every time Granny look out she smile. Was a happy smile but, like I say arready, tired.

But I have to admit dat she did prepare me little bit by little bit for what was comin to pass with she. She tell me dat was no different from de sun goin down an I shouldn worry cos she was arready risin, like dat selfsame sun, in me.

I does still cry when I think of it, but soon after I 'member de fight dat Missa Coleridge fight to keep all dat concrete standin. Jacob fadder tell we how de floor of de dancin hall jus split apart so slow you barely notice it. An den it was a snorin, gapin hole like de sea dat Moses part with he own little piece o laughin stick. Dat take a coupla years. An den it was de bungalow he call de King Room dat crack up like biscuit an start crumblin. An den everyting else start fallin down.

Joan fadder say dat he was by de swimmin pool when de water start to leak. He say he was de one dat empty de pool which shoudda empty from ever since, cos no more touris was comin dere. Jacob fadder say Joan fadder lie. Was he who see Missa Coleridge eye turn glass an his face go red like if de finger o God was on he throat an chokin im, when he see de sight o de root of dat laughin tree peepin out de bottom o he swimmin pool. And in a funny way I tell meself dat really was Granny hand. Coleridge look up at we little maggabone house on top de hill and was as if he see de tree for de first time.

Jacob fadder say dat he was standin by where de gate used to be when he catch sight o Coleridge runnin up de hill 'at a vory, vory forst rate.' (He start practisin to speak like Coleridge from de time he turn watchman.) 'But was onforchnate for Coleridge because soon as he foot hit de road is attack he heart attack im'.

Well it had a whole heap o confusion an confabulation after dat. An talk didn finish till long time after govment deport Coleridge body back to he famly in Englan.

But quiet come and a whole heap o realisin follow after dat.

Now I is many tings but one ting I is definitely not, is agriculturally botanical in my knowledge. But Cyril (by now I learn dat pretty fella name yuh see?) Cyril siddown on de chair dat Granny uses to sit on, an he explain everyting to me.

He say de laughin tree is a collokyalizam (yep! he know big wud too) for a special tree from de mountain where my Granny come from when she was young. An dat tree grow down more dan it grow up. It does push down root like if it tryin to reach de navel o de earth. It don have no respect for rock an stone eider. It does break through dem if it have ter. Dat tree jus keep pushin till it hit a table full o water (I didn ask im to explain dat cos I didn want him to tink I ignorant) which he say, is always dere below de ground, even in dese dry parts where we live. Once dat root reach, it start drinkin like Coleridge tourist used to drink deir funnylookin drink from straw. It drink so much dat it start to fatten up an spread an sweat through every leaf an branch. De sweatin is de laughin. An I have it from good autoritarianism, my Cyril imself, dat is so tree does laugh.

My Cyril say dat de trouble does start when dem root on de side o de laughin tree start to spread out an run. Is a tree dat curious an a little bit aggressive (he kinda look at me an smile). It just mash through anyting dat in it way, which is what Missa Coleridge find out jus before he heart attack im.

An yunno what de best part was? Well, my Cyril say dat soon as dat centre root siddown at dat table o water down dere to drink, a laughin tree don care what happenin on top. You chop it an you burn it, you kick it an you cuss it; it jus cyahn dead. Dat's what my Cyril say.

Well, it still upset me little bit when he mention chop an burn; an I had to ask im. When he say, 'Whatsimatter, girl?' I had to ask im:

'Cryil? Why de hell I goin to wan to chop-an-burn a tree dat my Granny bury under?'

A Way to Catch the Dust

For Binéta

'Something the sea says (deep in my night of blood)

That morning, Mantos of the parched skin, the Old Testament face, leaves his house - the one that sits like a mound of earth above the bay - and shuffles up, once again, to the edge of the precipice that looks directly out to sea.

He will be up there all day. Will lick a thumb from time to time, hold it to the air and count to nine exactly. Then withdrawing his hand he will close his eyes and rub his thumb against his index finger as if he were listening for something that those fingers ought to tell him.

For the past five days, he has been feeling the eyes of the young man on his back, from the moment he begins the slow climb up the stony track past the white graveyard of lambi shells, past the arched and sloping patches of brush and mint grass to the small clearing on the precipice. And even when he cast his eyes over the hill-hugging sage and borbook and does not see the white shirt, the lean and curiously angular

113

shape against the black sand of the bay, he knows that the youth is somewhere down there - amongst the houses, the decaying boats, the ailing coconut trees - looking up at him.

That awareness used to worry him. But now, not even the unsettling curiosity of a peculiar young man could distract him from his tiring morning climb up to the lip of this precipice from where he will send out a hand from time to time to feel the wind, or a tongue in a tentative attempt to taste it. For it is not a normal wind, not the gritty, warning winds of an ordinary hurricane which are always followed by a familiar stillness a couple of days or so before it arrives. Those he knows the tastes and textures of and would, in passing, warn the village a couple of weeks before they hit. 'Storm coming. Hold yer boats and brace yerself.'

And almost before he'd finished speaking, the bracing would begin. The men would drag their boats further up the sand and chain them against anything they hoped would hold. They strengthened houses, replaced old pillars and caulked the crevices of their homes the way they would a craft. And they waited with the same certainty with which he'd warned them; since they had already learnt - a long time back - that he was not called The Wind Taster for nothing.

It is this certainty, more than anything - he believes - that young Simon Coper wants: how to taste the wind and *know*. Still, if the youth worries him, this wind disquiets him even more because it has no taste. What it carries is an odour and a colour.

In his mind it is a wide, yellow wind and he believes he knows it: how in the first few days it will nibble at the land - a steady, intent grazing - and then in the final days, the week he called the Dry White Time, it will begin to release the dust. Strange dust, fine as air and gold, the colour of ground corn, deposited like a whisper on the poisonous green of the red mangroves that darken the southern fringes of the bay, that settles in the cracked bark of the aged sea grape trees and the rotting grooves of the ancient, patient wooden houses crouched like so many sightless crabs on the slopes, with their backs turned to the sea.

There, it will drop a load more subtle than the taste of sea or the smell of other lands - the barely visible corn-yellow clouds it shifts.

It will also poke a finger in his mind and lift the skirt of memories: a storm, a rising, curling wave, a naked girl - dark as the sand on their beach with a voice so soft, so hoarse, he still remembered it. Though, the last time he heard it, it was sad and tight with tears and hurt.

That thought of her - the memory of her voice quietens his fear of the boy, the way the dark eyes follow him, the wordless shadowing by the angular shape even when he stands down there on the crowded beach watching the young men wrestle with each other and the waves.

Mantos has also learnt to be wary of this wind as much as he has come to fear the boy. It is brighter up there on the cliff. The little light that rains down from the sky seems to be sucked in by the sand. He looks for the white shirt amongst the houses, at the edges of the mangrove; then thinks of the girl, mutters a name and makes himself feel better.

The bay has assumed the greyness of the sea. Perhaps sensing something in the day, the boats have come in early. The men and their scrawny families are ragged, moving bits of windswept colour against the naked beach. Every now and then they shift their heads his way. And he could hear their voices, imagine their deep-throated, uneasy chuckles. In the past few days they have seen him climb the hill too often and stay up there too long.

Simon Coper is not amongst them. If he were, they would barely look at him. They hardly ever look at him these days, except Meena Farrow whose unblinking eyes would not leave his face. Those eyes would follow his retreating shirt as if tethered to him by hate - that is, until he turned around and something in his eyes repelled her.

The sky is a wound when Mantos decides, reluctantly, to leave the hill, resentful of the very idea of the long walk down, the slipping, small white stones that seem to gather on the slope by the minute.

ooooooo

The beach is empty now. He looks to the swamps where the dull stretch of water disappears beneath the cramped branches like a dark amorphous road, expecting to see a shape there, a white shirt. It was into that darkness that he'd seen the white shirt disappear six months ago. It was carrying a bundle then.

And on emerging empty-handed from between the tangled embrace of mangrove, the boy had stopped, surprised to see him up there, another, darker shape against the sky looking down on him.

Although he could not see it, he was sure the boy had smiled, as if to say that the fact of being caught out there, just the two of them - in a mist of rain - made them both equal sharers of an awful secret. It was the carelessness with which he turned away and took the track through the houses that Mantos remembers now. And the terrible thing was that he had kept the secret. Had said nothing when they discovered the body of the girl cradled between some roots in the very heart of the mangroves. That was after a week and a half of searching until their noses had finally guided them to her.

They said it was like a nest in there, the kind that hawks and ground-doves built - without a roof and lined with rags and sticks and straw. They all thought she was asleep at first, her body folded with a restfulness she'd never had in life. They would never know what the boy had done to her, for they were too fearful to find out. The shapelessness of the wrapping, its unnatural contours had warned them of a horror that it was better that their eyes did not behold. So they put her to rest that way.

What turned their suspicion - and Meena Farrow's hate - on the boy was not so much what they *knew* for sure as what they thought him capable of. The girl was a poison to the boy. They all knew that. She despised and cursed him for his awkwardness, his silence, the fact that - skinful of bones that he was - he could never pull an oar as easily as a real man ought to. Nor would he ever wrestle with a wave like they could. And, worst of all, he did not have the balls or wit to answer her. He just offered her that dried-out smile that wasn't a smile at all, which merely stretched his lips and kept those eyes fixed on her with a strange, unwavering interest.

I never did like dat girl. Mantos cast a last glance at the sky as if expecting to catch a glimpse of Meena Farrow's daughter there: short, pretty and compact, with the bright and laughing eyes of a baby and a tongue as sharp as hooks. Her smile used to be like that too, sweet until her laughter came. *I did never like she.*

He has repeated those last words more often than he cares to remember, after blaming her of course for her own death, for the impulse that had made him climb the hill that evening and catch sight of a boy disappearing and then emerging from the mangrove. He even blamed her for his own dislike of her which he believed accounted for his not speaking at the time especially the evening the police came.

The boy's eyes were on him all the time. He placed himself against the trunk of an old grape tree, folded his arms and waited while the two policemen examined the sand that the sea had smoothed over a million times, stared at the darkening patch of mangroves, then at their faces and shrugged. He could still see the thin face, the broad forehead that glistened - even in the fading day - and those small and curiously obsidian eyes that were all the more unsettling because they did not blink behind his glasses. And there had been no fear there.

The policeman who did all the talking mumbled his astonishment that something like *that* could happen at all in a place like *this*. He asked a couple of disinterested questions to which there had been no answer really. *Why would anyone do a thing like that? What was the point in folding her up so carefully? Nobody didn launch a new boat recently?* At that point he examined the beached crafts with narrowed eyes. *Or, did the village owe the sea something - a life perhaps?* His eyes surveyed their faces for a while, like an uncertain hand rummaging beneath stones for whelks, and somewhere between their outraged silence and Meena Farrow's sobs, he muttered something to his friend, turned and left as abruptly as he came.

'It have some things a pusson shouldn, couldn hold inside fo long.' Mantos fingers the air unhappily, 'Like somebody else's crime. It means dat, in some way, you begin to own it. Perhaps Simon Coper also know dat'.

After a couple of weeks, it was simply too late. He could not say it. He thought of the way they would have looked at him then, the questions in their eyes - questions that he'd also asked himself. Why did he keep it from them for so long? Why didn't he tell the police when they asked, or when Meena Farrow needed confirmation of what everyone else suspected. How many times had the boy, with that little smile of his, come up to him and greeted him since? As aware now of his power, as the wrestlers on the beach were of their strength.

If people did not have the habit of avoiding Simon Coper, of not *looking*, they would see the admission in his eyes. They would notice how it modified him and how, in turn, it changed the way they were with him. For there was now a stiffening in his presence. His arrival muted conversations and dampened laughter. It made them leave the beach and head for home earlier than they used to. They could go on avoiding him, but they could no longer pretend he was not there.

It was not long after that, that the youth began to follow him. To speak to him. To insist, 'Make me know de weather, Ole Fella - I want to be like you.'

'Can't be like nobody except yuhself. And!' His voice stumbled over an anger that, hitherto, he had not been aware of, 'And me! I suttinly don't want to be like you.'

'I - I kin be anything I wan to be.'

'An do anything yuh wan to do? An *tink* you get away with it? Like, like -' But he could not bring himself to say it. Reminding the boy of what he had seen him do was also reminding himself of what he should have done. 'That's the trouble with you, young fella. I should ha..'.

'Should ha what!'

Mantos remembers looking at the hard face and thinking that he might have been a fine young man had it not been for the too-tight forehead, the too-small, too-dark eyes magnified a couple of times behind those glasses and the unbearable thinness that he carries like an illness.

But he has also seen worse, those who do not have the fine dark skin of this youth, the tight-lipped awareness; did not have half his education. And, to them, life had been much kinder.

What is it about him? Perhaps it is the secret way he moves, the way he carries his body like he does not own it - as if every movement of his limbs was a denial of his right to open spaces. The fact that even when this odd and angry boy does something with the others, he has an air of looking on. He makes no attempt to own the world and so all the world disowns him.

'Leave me in peace. Don wan to have nutting to do with you.'

'Teach me to read the wind.'

'You don read de wind - you taste it.'

'Den teach me how to taste it.'

'You got a tongue, not so?' Mantos spat at the sea and as he walked away he could feel the boy's smile on his back.

That smile had changed the last time Simon Coper approached him, or rather he'd jumped out in front of him, from somewhere amongst the boats, and startled him.

' I know what you trying to catch up there with your finger point up like dis.' The boy held up a thumb to his face and stared scornfully at it. 'You tryin to catch a cold.'

'You little murdering sonuvabitch. You got a heap o jumbie in yuh head, an you not goin get rid of dem on me. Is mad you mad, y'hear me? You is a flippin crazy man.' That wiped the smile off his face as if a light was switched off inside of him. What replaced it was a stillness and that same interested look he'd shown in little Margaret Farrow the time before he killed her.

Mantos watches the light, trying to push the boy out of his mind. His eyes wander on the seabirds coming in, especially the dark ones with the great unmoving wings as wide as sails. They seem to appear from the heart of the hovering clouds, their flight so smooth it is almost dreamlike, propelled it seemed, not by movement but by the subtle shifting of their will. Birds - ocean birds - birds that hated land are gathering on the branches of the grapes and mangroves like a host of animated blooms. As if seeking confirmation, the old man studies the gathering flock. Amongst the bright white ones that always arrive in larger numbers and the smaller greys, he spots a couple that he was partly hoping would not be there: white everywhere except at the top of their night-black wings, the edges of which are outlined with white feathers, like chalk-marks on a stone.

'Brace y'all self,' he mutters irritably, glaring at the boats, the houses, and the silent bay. This time, he will keep his warning to himself.

He has his reasons. He has his reasons for not passing them a warning this time. And if, afterwards, they ever ask him why, he will remind them of a girl and what their people did to her. And why - why, he remains always as deeply unforgiving as the sea.

Mantos is now as certain of the nature of the storm before him as he is of the intentions of the boy. There was a time when their reliance on his words gave him a certain kind of pleasure. A power even, that sat on a knowledge that used to be the property of everyone. The power that a mad young man observed in him and now wants badly enough to kill him for.

He has seen how, over the years, they allowed their instincts to be dulled by the assurance of his presence. A laziness crept in - a carelessness he cultivated in them over all these years.

For there are signs - things they ought to see and hear themselves - that should be enough to warn them. There, past the gurgling white hillocks of lambi shells - now a pink and quiet graveyard in the strange light - past the terrible waste and the awful smell of swamp, past the Point of Shadows, is the rock they used to call The Sound - a jagged chunk of granite that rears its mighty head out of the water and straddles the air like some horned beast. Its great, twisted mouth is turned up at an angle to the sky in a timeless scream that remains silent even in the murderous hurricanes which, from time to time, sweep in from the north and west. It is the East storms - terrible and rare - that give The Sound a voice. And the night before, it began to 'sing' - a low hum, like a breath across the mouth of a bottle.

There is also the beach. He stares across the water and then down at the grey babbling mess of waves kicking against the shore. For days the ocean has been emptying its stomach in the bay. The black beach, whose crisp, crystalline sand would, in daylight, glitter like stars against a midnight sky, is dull and barely recognisable. It is strewn with piles of wood, algae and canvas bags that are weighted around the sides with chunks of lead. In his time they would gather the bags and burn them when the weather eased, or one of the young men would go past a few horizons and return them to the sea where the waves would reclaim what had once been the clothing for the corpses of white men. In his time, they would see all this, know what it meant and begin to brace themselves.

And for this kind of storm, the bracing would be much deeper. It would happen in the bones, in the narrowing of the eyes at the giant swathe of light that seeped like a wound in the lower reaches of the sky. In the way the women's hands supported hips as large as hulls or thin as oar blades. In the uneasy glances of the men. And by the time it arrived, they would be prepared.

ooooooo

A hard wind comes off the water and slaps him in the face. It leaves an aftertaste of salt and bitterness. Mantos pulls his shirt closer and readies himself to climb down the hill.

Just as he is about to turn, he feels something hard, like the limbs of a crab against his neck. And then the voice - the soft chuckle at the back of it, that is both a mockery and a threat. 'I *catch* you, ole fella.'

For the first time Mantos becomes aware of the fall below: the waiting rocks, the wet and writhing mouth of the sea. He shudders, feels as if the cliff has moved beneath his feet. He tries to step back but the hand of the boy is strong.

Mantos closes his eyes. He could hear the birds across the bay, their sudden agitation. And then like a quick release of wings, the fear he had been carrying all these months leaves him.

'Well,' he breathes, his tongue flickering like a sudden, nervous flame against the dryness of his lips. 'You *catch* me for true.' Something tells him that he must not show his terror to this boy; that, like a mangue-fly that feeds on blood and poison the youth will grow strong on it.

The old man is greeted with a soft laugh. He wonders how the youth has done it - climbed up the path so quietly that he did not hear him. Nor did Mantos even catch a glimpse of the white shirt at the corner of his eye.

They are alone out here - exactly like that last time he saw him with the girl - in the remnants of a day that has begun to trickle down the sky and stain the water red.

The gulls have quickly settled down again in a quiet huddle amongst the trees. *Brace yuhself,* he thinks, shaping the words with quivering lips, cringing at the new meaning they have suddenly, unexpectedly assumed for him.

The weight of the hand has grown around his neck. All he hears now is the boy's breathing. A sudden irrational conviction seizes Mantos, if only he could turn around, see his eyes, face him he... but then the thought of falling backwards is much worse.

'What you want to know, sonny?'

'Everything!'

'Like -like, uh-' Mantos says what comes first to mind - what in a way, lay at the heart of his entire life. 'Like how to catch de dust?'

'De?'

'Yes - is all around you, everywhere - de dust. You let me go. I show you.'

'You mad.'

'Yes - no.' He quickly licks a thumb and holds it to the wind. His lips, from habit, shapes the numbers - one to nine exactly. Just as quickly and without turning, he pushes his hand behind him. 'Pass your hand across dis finger.'

There is a movement from the boy, an increased pressure on his neck. 'Pass it!' He mutters thickly, 'You *say* you wan to know everything!'

The pressure eases and he feels a hard, dry finger brush his thumb.

Mantos waits, hoping that Simon Coper has the kind of fingers that could feel the film of dust. Not everyone could. The boy withdraws his hand abruptly and the old man flinches. He bows his head and braces himself. Then he sees the arm thrust forth in front of him, the thumb glistening with spittle.

'No, too much,' he mumbles, staring at the shining thumb. 'Not *too* much!'

'You turn the finger round like dat.' Cautiously, he takes the boy's wrist and turns. The hand does not resist him. He glances round at the face, dark against an even darker sky. He realises the youth's eyes are closed, the narrow nostrils flared as though prised wider by the wind. It occurs to Mantos that this is his moment. There will never be a better time to escape this boy - this shadow that has attached itself to him. He feels strong enough to do it, to spin him around and throw him.

The thought must have communicated itself to the youth because he opens his eyes suddenly as if startled out of sleep. He remains surprisingly relaxed. Mantos sees the curiosity in his eyes, the dare that is also a desire and he realises that if he has lost his moment, the boy's compulsion to kill him has also passed.

The old man feels himself relax.

'Come!' He lifts his eyes to the first flush of lightning down the edges of the sky. 'C'mon,' he says again, more urgently this time. 'Lemme show you how to do it.'

It has taken him more than four times the years this boy has lived - to learn to catch the dust, first to know that it was there at all and then, years later, to find a way to retrieve it.

And now, here he is, on a precipice above the sea, beneath a purpling sky, trying to teach an insane boy, in minutes, a secret that it has taken him a lifetime to work out: *just the right amount of moisture on the thumb. No - not too long because the finger will dry and the wind will take back its dust.* Don't make the thumb too flat either, because the dust will never settle. In fact it has to be at an angle so exact, he is amazed at himself that he had ever learnt it.

All this he does with a quiet, focused urgency. For he can feel the coming storm like the breath of a beast against the ear. And now there is the faint and distant smell of rot. That awareness releases him completely of his first, numbing rush of fear. Soon the rain will come and there will be no difference between earth and air - just a wilful, driving violence in which no living thing should find itself.

The boy has discovered the dust at last. It shows on his face. The satisfaction of a secret shared, of reaching for what, before, had not been there and grasping it. But it is not enough for him. This discovery is too small to be a miracle, and - once a person learns to do it - too predictable to be a trick. It is also a gesture that leads to nothing, that offers no release from anything. It confirms or denies nothing.

The boy's face is a mask in the decaying light but Mantos senses his dissatisfaction. How can he begin to tell him, to make him understand, that these little grains of air are like doorways to a time that exists only in his mind now, and above all to a woman with a voice as hoarse as drums? That it is what confirms she once existed?

Up here with a storm over their shoulders, the boy is just a frail face, propped up by an even frailer frame - a human who had every limb in place but who, somehow, still appears mal-formed. Like one of those solitary etchings a person sometimes encounters on the sand. All you would ever know about it, was that it was drawn by the hands of a child, who must have, in leaving it to the will of the wind and sea, acknowledged the one abiding law of life. That it would not last forever.

It is an impression that had no validity beyond that moment. The old man has simply decided that this young man's very present need matters more than his history, or what he really is. Mantos has no doubt that if he lives beyond this day he will continue to hate him.

'I used to think you ugly,' he begins cautiously. In the dimming light he can barely see the face. If the boy is hearing him, he shows no sign. The peculiar stillness is there once more. Only this time he is standing in a light that reveals no details, no expression. He is a *bois-bois* boy - one of the stick-people that adults make and stuff with straw for children to tear and strike at.

'Right now, I don't tink so. If people think you no use to nobody, especially yourself, is because you believe you is. What *make* you come like dat, what make you hate so stupid dat you have to kill a girl to show it? Me - you think I *like* dem? You think -' He pulls his collar around his ears more to protect himself from the storm that has suddenly risen inside his head.

'I'll tell you why this storm will come and dey wouldn believe *what* hit dem. Why I prepare dem for every wind dat blow, every livin drip o rain. Why I been preparin dem all dis time, so dat dey will never be ready for dis one when it come.

I been waitin for dis storm, sonny. Like I been waitin all my life.' His arms took in the sky the wind, the sea, 'Dis storm is de one dat bring de girl, last time.' He chuckles harshly, bitterly and eyes the shape with pleasure. It feels like the first time in years that he has allowed himself to laugh - a real release that changes his voice and makes him somehow younger.

'De?'

'Y'hear me right - de girl. A hurricane is a sneeze. A little fit o temper, compare to what is about to come. Dis - dis one is a stinkin, kickin rage.

'I have more reason to hate dem dan you could ever have. I been doin dat for de best part o my life. De best part! But like I say, it never give me no reason to go out dere and kill one of deir own.'

The boy's shirt rustles in the twilight like the wings of a disturbed bird.

If now, Mantos speaks as if they were apart from those below, it is because two moments of bad weather have made them so - those and the single thing he feels he shares with this stranger boy who, a while ago, was prepared to kill him. A silence and a grief he has carried for years that were sometimes so unbearable he would not leave his house for days.

'I tell you a story,' he mutters quietly. 'And I don expect you to believe it. But is true as dis living dust around us. Sometimes I think of it meself, and it feel like a dream now - like some creature dat settle down once inside my mind and make a little nest in dere, and now it gone to sleep for good. It don't feel like it real no more. De only proof I got is this - de dust.

I is eighty now - yunno dat? De last of what y'all call De Old Ones. Me an Maisie Green. But I used to be young too - young and empty handed but mih head was full o dreams. It have a time in a pusson life when you don't believe you'll ever die - all dat hope, all dat life! You so full of it, all you see is a brightness in front of you dat blind you to everyting else. I never had de chance to be like dat - young an strong an feedin on de bread of hope. And you - you should unnerstan dat. Cos you was never young. Dem never give you o me a chance to be.

Yuh see, my mother got me from a man nobody never meet. Or if dem ever meet him she never tell dem it was he. Somewhere in dem hills above dere mongst de mapou and de mist she lay down with a forest man - not sea.

I dunno what it was dat make her keep dat silence - shame, o pride, o love, o perhaps all of dem mix up. I dunno. Anyway, he fill her up not just with me but with dat selfsame silence dese forest people carry all de time with dem. I born dat way - with all dat silence in mih blood and something else: a sort o knowledge o de world, de little tings - de way a leaf does curl, the colour of de veins on dem, de shape of a bird wing, how a seagull spread it toes. I could hear de crabs under de sand; the turning of de worms. Was like if dat forest man carry all he learning in he seed, like it was also blood. And he pass dat on to me.

Once she tell me I was jus like him. Was de only time she mention im, and dat time was a warning dat in dis place if you different den you good as dead.'

Mantos laughs a shrill, dry laugh.

'Now take a child dat could point a finger at de sea an say exactly where de fish is and what kind o fish it have out dere. Or throw an eye at what de wave bring in de night before and say what kind o weather dat goin mean tomorrow. Now dere aint no place for dat. No explainin. An de only ting dat nobody can't explain is de work o de devil. So I become to dem a devil chile. Something dat possess my mother in de bush dat dey had to get rid of. An worse, my mother had no place mongst dem. From de time she got me in dis funny way she wasn human no more. A thing was what she was, who hardly talk to nobody. Young and full o flesh and lovin only de child she pick up from a stranger in de forest, she was de bait for any nasty man who decide to lay a claim to her.

It start with a man name Randolf Groner who threaten he would take me out, tie a stone around mih neck an drop me in de sea if she didn give sheself to im. He come to my mother all de time - nights, late, when nobody couldn see im. He come and he call er out. And she always go, knowin dat if she didn he was goin to keep he word.

I could hear dem fightin in de dark out dere. She beggin im to leave er alone - jus dis time, for once. An little as I was I know dat, dat beggin an fightin was for me. I 'member one night between cryin, she lay down by me and try to explain everyting. How difference for we people is like school children with a snake. Dey either run from it or kill it. And I tell her dat mebbe de snake should try to run from dem. Some snake she tell me, just don know where to run to.

It went on for years. Sometimes another man come to replace Randolf Groner. And she would always go out.

I was fourteen when she went out for de last time. Dis time it wasn a man dat call her out. She just went an didn come back. And in de same way I did know when de sea was goin to send some rain, I get up dat mornin, didn see her dere, and know she wasn't comin back.

I s'pose dat what protect me was deir shame when, a coupla days after, dey lift she body off de tide. Dat an de fact dat she did prepare me for it. Every night she come back in dat house she tell me what I must and musn't do. Why I should abide my time. Why, to protect meself from dem, I must teach meself a kind o blindness, kill de smells dat nobody else could smell, shut down my hearing like you bolt a door. And wait.

But waitin tire you out and sometimes yuh mind force you to forget. Not what happen - I could never forget dat - or how, or even why, but all de nasty tings dat go wid it. De hurtin an de hate.

But then, you see, ignorance is a beast with a stomach like de sea - it always hungry, and it feed on anyting. No matter how much my mother prepare me, no matter dat I grow up mongst dem, no matter how much like dem I did become, she didn prepare me for one ting: nobody would have me for deir daughter.'

The boy makes as if to speak, but Mantos stops him with a quick impatient gesture. Now that he has started he simply wants to finish. The youth has become something to talk at - a rare and listening presence.

'Yuh see, Killer Boy, I was de child o de woman dat lay down wit a demon in de mountains. Dat mean I carry his seed, and dey believe dat seed must die in me.

Hah! Ain't got no loneliness more worse dan dat! Ain't got no knowledge more bitterer dan dat - dat yuh life stop with you, dat you will not live *past* yourself. Dat in de end when you shut yuh eyes for good, you ain got nothing left to show for it. Dat de world end with you.

But you can't strangle water; you can't close yuh fist around it an hold on to it for good. Water always find a way. And life - life is like dat. Life always find a way to make room for itself. And life did make a little room for me.

It come in de form of a girl. And to dis day, I believe was a storm like dis dat bring her. Dey don't come regular, dese storm. I see three in my whole life and I count meself cursed or p'raps lucky because some people live and never see one. De first one come when I was a child and I don't remember much of it, except a smell and a old woman name Androvy passing a tongue across mih finger and holdin it up to de wind.

De second time I recognise de coming by de smell - a smell dat was so small and far, you hardly know it there, de smell o sweat an dirt an breathin, like people livin in a tight, small place - in a sort of rockin darkness.

It wake up all de tings I believe dat I did bury in mihself, de tings my mother encourage me to stifle. I feel it weeks before it reach, like a blind man feel somebody presence in a room. And I warn dem. I dunno why. Perhaps was to show dem dat what I born with was not so bad. Dat it could serve some good. Dat was hardly different from a man who could pull a bigger net or lean harder on an oar. Dat *if* I was different, I had no say in it.

I dunno. Dem didn lissen at first - thought was my madness for a woman dat gone to my head.

But den about a week after, dey start seein de message dat de sea start leavin on de sand.

You see in my time people really *know* de sea. Dem know dat de ocean have three parts. And every part is like a world dat complete to itself. All we see from here is de part with all dat light, all dat blue. And for most of us, dat's all we know. Past that - further out, you got another kind o deep. Is de place o shark and whale and big squid, and de fast fish: mackerel, tuna, marlin.

And den past all dat still, you have de dark. De bowels o de ocean.

Is like a bad dream down dere. Ain't got no light down dere. Hardly got no bottom. Hardly got no life. And what life it got down dere is like nothing dat you ever see. Fish dat ain't got no eye. Creatures dat carry deir own light under deir skin, or hold it like a torch on top deir head. A kind o worm dat got root like grass, brown on top an white below. You smell it and it smell o sulphur. You burn it an it dont want to burn. And other livin things, pink and soft like your tongue - creatures who' whole body is a mouth. How I know?

Is what y'all ignorance been walkin over since last week on dat beach down dere. Is what I didn show nobody dis time. An lemme tell you someting else, Sweet Man, anyting dat kin reach dat deep to upset de stomach o de sea can't be good for us.

Besides,' this he mutters quietly, softly, 'Besides Fatimi tell me. Dat was how I know was out o all dat darkness dat she come.'

He looks at the boy uncertainly, the quivering lips holding the shape of the last word. 'No! Wasn't no mermaid. Unless de sea have black ones too with foot and hair like me. Was a real girl - flesh and blood and warm like you - an dat sea deliver her to me. Maisie Green will tell yer. God blind her for de part she play in what happen afterwards.

De night de storm reach, I decide to walk out to de bay an meet it - yes! Was what I decide. Only it didn have no bay out dere no more. I decide to go out dere and face it; cos nothin didn mean a lot to me no more. My life, I was thinkin, didn have no worth. So what difference if a East storm tek it. My mother didn hardly go no different - so?

I dunno how long I was out dere for. What protect me was de way de wind was comin cross dis cliff - sort of bouncing off and missin us down below.

I was watching de wind distress de sea, thinkin - thinkin dat p'raps dis was de end o de world, dat maybe was not fire dat would take we an dis wicked world in de end but water. All dat water!

I was talkin to meself, cussin de wind, de rain, de whole dam world an laughing. Yes was madness but I welcome it - cos madness mek me happy for de first time.

ooooooo

She come on de curl of a wave. On de top of it. Like you was sitting on de edge of a movin, rollin cliff that lift you up and rest you down right dere on de ground in front o me. I didn *see* her come. I figure dat out by de way she just appear. It had to be de only way.

A girl - naked as de night, and just as dark. Standin dere in front o me, tremblin from de wet. She must ha say someting, ask for help, tell me hello - *something*. I dunno. I notice de voice straight away, soft like if it come from inside mih head. She didn speak like we speak and I couldn see her proper. Except dat she was slim an tall and she was in a bad way, like she was goin to fall down any minute. I didn think about de confusion in my head - all de question dat start poppin up straightaway. Mebbe she was one o dem foreigners in a boat out dere with other people, and de storm drag dat boat from under dem. How she manage to swim across dat kind o sea - well, miracle does happen, not so?

My heart was goin like ah engine. I wasn thinkin, I wasn even frighten. I jus know I had to bring her in de house an dry her out. Which is exactly what I do.'

Mantos lifts his head and stares at the boy who is hugging himself against the wind.

'Don think I didn tell meself dat I was mad or dreamin. Dat mebbe my distress fly up in mih head an make a woman out of air for me. But if it was distress I was dam well glad to stay distress de rest o me life.

But - but you see, she had weight an voice an warmth. An when I carry her up de hill, de little light from de sky fall on she face and I see dat she was one o we.

I fix a bed proper on de floor for her. I do all dis in de dark and with de lightning dat come through de house from time to time. Don ask me why. It jus didn feel proper to light no light. And soon as I finish, before I could blink me eye she gone to sleep.

Dat night I sit down on de floor an watch her for a while - as much as de little bit o lightning allow me - wonderin who she was, where she might ha come from. And how - how *anybody* could come out of dat kind o sea alive. I fall alseep sittin on de floor wit my head full up of all dem tings.

Next day I wake up to a clean day. De whole world look chastise - flat an mash up and everyting turn upside down or wrong-side out.

Before I step out, I look on de floor to see if it was really dream dat I was dreamin durin de night dat pass. In a way I was sort of hopin dat I was. Or at least, *iffen* I wasn dreamin I was expectin dat whatever it was I meet out dere last night did pass way wit de passin o de storm.

She was still dere lyin on de floor. Still sleepin. Now I could see her better, I see how dark an smooth she was. Hardly any hair. Cut low on she head like a boy. She face - I never see nobody so pretty - was long an slim an *quiet*. A face you couldn read. Everyting bout her was slim an long, an smooth. It had three little mark right dere.' Mantos brushes his left cheek with his fingers. 'Just under de bone, like three little fish you lay down one on top de other. I never see a pusson so perfect. Is dat what make me fraid, not de strange way dat she come, not even how I was goin to explain her to everybody else. Was de perfectness o dat girl.

I think about it all day and I realise dat I had a problem. I couldn tell dem dat I bring her from somewhere else. I could hear dem wonderin, how come she didn speak no language dat nobody else round here know? How come dey didn see her de day before de storm? I think o hidin her but it strike me dat I had to make her understand why first and I didn know how I was goin to do dat.

I glad I never try to hide her because I realise afterwards dat she didn like to be cover up by nothing. Dat was one of de two tings dat was really bad for her. De other ting - *what* dey use against us in de end was, well... I'll tell you when I come to it.

On top of all o dat she was different, never mind de short hair and dem little mark on she face. A pusson could look de same like everybody else, but you know - and you dunno *how* you know - but you *know* if dem come from somewhere different.

Anyway, she give me almos a week to think bout it, cos dat was how long she sleep, like she was sleepin off de toil o centuries, wakin up only for me to feed her, or jus openin she eye to say someting I didn unnerstan.

I hardly go out meself - only a coupla times for dem to see dat I was alright. Nobody hardly uses to come to my place anyway.

People was out dere pulling deyself back together but all I want was to sit right dere on de floor with my door bolt up and feed my eyes on her. Sometimes she catch me lookin and she look straight back - not offerin nothing, not askin nothing, jus lookin back at me.

Love, sonny - love come easy when you empty an you needin it; it come easier when you got to tek care o somebody o someting you been wanting bad and never expect to get.

Love did come. And it was easy for both of us, cos some tings you don' need no language for.

And with it - with it come de terror of de *outside*. Perhaps she realise it long before me, dat I was afraid to take her out into de day. To let eyes fall on her. Mebbe dat was why she allow me to keep her in dere for so long, comin out with me only in de night and only for a little while. *Outside* - I realise dat I always been afraid of it. You see, *outside* was where my mother used to go. *Outside* was where she went one day an never come back home. *Outside* was a place dat hurt.

One mornin, must ha been a coupla weeks after she come, I decide to tek my boat, go out an catch some butterfish - she use to *like* butterfish. I tell er in mih prettiest English, 'Me - Mantos going return soon.' By then I know she name was Fatimi - leasways dat was how I hear it.

I went out there, got my fish and hurry back, and what I see?

She was standin in de yard with my sheet wrap around her and she had a fire goin. She make a fireside same like we make, preparin for when I come home, you see? I see her first an den I see de crowd. All of dem standin on de beach jus watchin an whisperin mongst demself while she goin bout her business like if dey wasn dere. Watchin er an whisperin like dem catch sight o something dat dey recognise but couldn unnerstan.

I was so fraid, I could ha faint. Fraid without hardly knowin why, except it was de same feelin dat settle in my stomach when bad weather about to come. Dat same night I try to warn er. I try to tell her dat I never want to see her near dem people, tell er what dey done to me.

Dat day I see someting else. I see de mark on she right shoulder. Dunno how I miss it befo, except perhaps was de first time I see all of her in proper daylight. A deep mark, like a burn you make in a pusson flesh, dat didn cure too well. De way children would dig de letters o deir name on de bark of a livin tree. A mark dat had no place on pretty skin like hers. A big 'L' dat sort of tie up itself wit ah 'C' - LC.

From dat time dey had their eyes on us. De fellas come to my house de way dey used to come to my mother. Only dis time dey come with jokes, with rum, with a basketful o fish dey claim dey bring for Fatimi to cook for all of us. But dem eyes was always on de doormouth of my house. On every movement dat she make. You could see de cravin in deir eyes, no matter how much dey try to hide it wid deir grin. Men, sonny, cravin what another man got just because he got it. Dey ask me question in all kind of funny way. Where a man could find a pretty woman so? It have more like she where she come from? How come she never talk? I always find some way to slip past de questions.

De women had a different way. They make deir children come sometimes and try to talk to her, and all she do was smile. Sometimes she answer dem in dat funny, pretty voice of hers. But it was not words to dem just sound dey didn unnerstan.

It continue, it continue, it continue - till tings get quiet and I thought dat mebbe, mebbe dem decide to leave two of us in peace.

I was a happy man. Except dem nights when Fatimi was tryin to say someting to me. I could hear de frighten in she voice, like it was de most important thing a pusson ought to know, but I jus couldn figure out what she was tryin to say to me. But I know dat it had something to do with de mark on she shoulder. In fact I had a feelin dat almos everyting had to do with dat mark, includin why she couldn stand lyin down in the darkness o de house for long. Why she reach for me, sometimes, bawlin like de devil was in front o she.

Times like those I hold on to her all through de night until it pass some time close to mornin. And it always lef me with a sadness - a deep-down, rockin darkness in me chest. That was how I know dat if I find out what dat mark is, I would know all about dat girl - who she was and where she come from, and why she come to me.

De trouble start with Maisie Green. She was young at de time and I s'pose till Fatimi come along she was de pretties woman for miles around. Dem fellas didn have no eyes for she no more. And Mason Joe, de fella she hope to married, jus jump a boat one day and lef she with a full belly an a empty hand. Jealousy s'not enough to explain what happen. S'like de little stone dat slip and start de landslide rollin. If dat stone didn slip - de landslide woulda happen anyway, but only a little bit later.

She spread word dat dat girl was a witch-woman - a mama malady. A demon-girl who come from nowhere and proof o de fact was dat she couldn speak no language known to human. Besides didn dey see de mark LC on she shoulder? LC stand for Lucifer Cometh. And me bein a demon child meself, was only natral dat I should go out and bring me own kind here. To mek it worse, she blame her for chasin Mason

Joe away. And when ole Miss Mertle Jones pass way dat same week she spread word dat Fatimi tief she soul.

Was de same ting when Rickman lose he boat on Trasher Reef - even if careless people been losin deir boat cross dere from ever since. And dat mark on she shoulder - she always went back to de mark on Fatimi shoulder - dat mark was suttingly de devil signature.

And den come de strike of seventy four when de islan stop sudden like a man who ketch a stroke and money didn have no value cos it didn have nothing to eat except fish for breakfast, tea an dinner.

Hard times does harden heart, sonny, and children aint no exception.

It begin wit dem children throwin stones at her - like dem used to do, come bois-bois time. I was never around for when it happen. I was too busy huntin food. And I tell meself now dat it was a good ting because, I would ha done worse dan you done to dat girl - tear all o dem little jookootoo rarse to pieces!

She keep it quiet - never tell me nothing till one day I come home and see her in de yard, she face swell up an she forehead bleedin. I look at her and I understand what happen straight away.

I went mad. I lose meself. Dis old rage dat been sleepin all dis while inside o me let loose and I couldn control it. I half-mash up a coupla houses, and start on dem boats, on de beach till something heavy knock me on de head an darkness fall on me.

Was de beginnin of a kind o war between us. A war without no words. Mornings I would get up and see a big cross paint on my door. Or salt spread out on de doorstep. And Maisie Green was always dere down on de beach keepin she eye on us.

I unnerstan for de first time what my mother mean when she tell me bout snake dat don't know where to run. What make *anybody* think it goin to be different somewhere else? What's de sense of runnin when you know you goin be runnin into de same ting dat you run from?

I didn wan to run, although I was close to it when dey discover de one weakness o de girl.

We was in de yard dat time, watchin dem watchin us. One o dem little chilren was playin with a tin pan, sort of knockin it on a stone and singing de way chilren who can't sing does sing. An every time she do dat, Fatimi jump. De chile, not knowing what he doing to her continue knockin dat pan harder on dat stone till my ooman couldn take de noise no more and she begin to scream. Mortal frighten she was. Mortal! It bring a grin to Maisie face and brighten dem pretty eyes o hers.

From den we didn have no rest, no day, no night. No rest. Everybody start knockin pan. Bucket too. Sometimes a piece o chain against a stone. And like dat dey try to drive my ooman mad.

I know she couldn take it for too much longer. Dat somehow it would kill her; and so I begin wishin for another storm, wave, o whatever it was dat bring her, to come an take she back. She got sick you see, wouldn eat no more, wouldn even talk to me.

Was one o dem days o rain - when you could hardly see anyting about you. One o dem drizzle days dat feel as if it never goin stop. I remember dat day so clear like I kin see it right dere in front o me cos dat was when Maisie an some children decide to come with a big oil drum in front my door an beat it like dey gone crazy. I left Fatimi curl up on de floor, coverin she ears and shoutin and I should ha pay attention to dat shoutin, cos before, she never use to shout, jus cry.

But all I was paying mind to was de murder in my heart when I unlatch de door to meet Maisie an dem chilren in my yard.

139

I didn realise it before, but over dem weeks, something did change in Maisie Green. I tell myself dat all dat hate she had inside she rise up to she skin an leave a ugliness dere. She was not a pretty woman any more. What was inside of her must have frighten it off. She was just a ragged, red-eye woman with a coupla teeth missin an I was about to kill her.

But I didn have no need to - a chip of de iron dat she been beatin dat drum so hard with just fly off and bury itself in she eye. I hear de scream and to dis day, I can't tell whether it come from Fatimi o she.

Dem chilren fly down de hill from frighten and I watch dat woman holdin she eye and rolling on de ground till she father come and lift she up and tek she home.

Fatimi was easy when I come in. Not smilin, jus staring at de roof as if something just done settle itself down inside o she. Mebbe she had something to do with it. I dunno. Mebbe.

Was a little time afterwards she look at me an tell me - in de best English you ever hear, 'Man, return soon.' Exactly as I used to tell she when I leave to go outside.

I figure dat she was tellin me what she always hear me say. Trying to make me laugh, perhaps. So I laugh, and she repeat it, serious. 'Mon return soon, Yantos. No cry.' Which was another thing I used to tell her. 'Don't cry Fati, don't cry.'

She say de same ting later in de night. Late. Dat night she didn sleep - would raise she head from time to time as if she was lisenin out for something. What I was seein dere in front o me was a different woman - no cry-cry girl dis time - but sure o sheself. Like what happen to Maisie make she realise or learn something dat make her more aware perhaps, and stronger too. I dunno.

I was half asleep when she got up - sudden so - de sheet droppin off of her de way a snake drop off it skin, and before I know it, she was runnin out in de rain down towards de beach.

Was a rising wind out dere and I could barely see because o dat flippin drizzle. But between my shoutin and runnin like mad to catch up with her, I see de shadow bobbing and weavin ahead o me like something in de mind. I didn hear no water splash, no sound o wings, no nothing - jus my name soft, so soft, Sonny, was like drizzle on a leaf.

And she was gone. Like dat!' The old man's palms explode against each other like a clap of thunder. The noise seems to awaken the youth. Mantos wonders if he has been listening at all, a question which leaves him with an odd sense of defeat.

'I- I didn kill her, Missa Mantos.' The youth's voice is a child's, frightened and unsure.

Irritably Mantos draws his shirt around him. 'I know you didn kill er. You wasn even born!'

'No! Not *yours*. *Her* - I didn—'

It is only when the youth steps back from him that Mantos realises that he has moved towards the boy. Simon Coper is angling his shoulders in the way a person would to protect his body from the force of a very strong wind. Only there is no wind now. Just an eerie stillness. Mantos has forgotten to watch the weather. They do not have much time up there. He knows this by the hollowness in his ears. The odd sensation of emptiness, as if the whole earth has sucked its breath in.

A sort of murky twilight has descended on the land, and inland where there were mountains before, there is only the darkness of descending clouds. This he watches critically. 'We have to go down. She goin strike us soon - sooner dan I expect.'

'I didn,' the boy persists.

'It don matter.' Again Mantos pulls his shirt around him in a half-hearted effort to shield himself from the chill that has risen in the air. He is tired and wants to go home. 'It done and it don't matter now. We have to go down from top of here, right now.'

The boy smiles - the old smile, the one he hates so much - and the old dislike, always so close under the skin, rises up again. To avoid the smile and spare himself the youth's half-hearted denial, the old man fixes his gaze on the area above the sea where, during all his days of watching, the sky has dripped with colours. It is a dirty churning grey there now.

People, he thinks, deny things when they have no need to. Like that boy is doing now. Denial is a kind of lie - the worse kind, because a person is doing it to himself. Everybody lies, like those folks down there who have been doing it all their lives. It is something that guilt requires. For guilt is a stone on which they are all now forced to sleep. And in a way it makes sense for them to reach for something softer.

'She'll come tonight,' he mutters. 'Sure as dat storm comin, Fatimi goin to come.' He lifts defeated eyes at the boy. 'And she wouldn change - like me. Age have no meanin for de ones like her. De ones dat come with de dust. De ones dat got away.'

'You never tell me where she come from.'

'De rockin darkness.'

'De?'

'I -I don expect you to believe me,' he adds quickly. 'But - since you ask me I goin tell you.'

'*Mon return soon* was what she say. Well after a lot o thinkin, I take dem words to Kanvi - dat village dat face de sea on de other side o here. You know Kanvi people, dem got a knowledge dat none o we ain' got no more. A pussnal knowledge o de sea. De woman who show me de way to catch de dust was from dere.

Had a fella dere name Winger. Winger know everyting. Used to be a teacher till book knowledge drive im mad. I take dem words to him cos dey never leave mih head. Sometimes you not s'pose to lissen to de words a pusson say, cos dat's not where you find de meanin, you find de meanin in de voice - Uh mean, de feelins dat de words come wrap in.

Fatimi was vex, you see - vex in a way dat frighten me, like she gone to prepare sheself to come again. P'raps dat was what she was tryin to tell me all dat time. An dis time - *dis time!* dey wouldn mek her leave so easy.

Man return soon - Winger couldn believe me first time when I say dem words, specially when I tell im bout de mark pon she shoulder. He ask me for she name, de way she look, other words she say. I search mih head and I remember some: *Jerry jef - tooky - nub. Mon nub Mantos* - she always use to say dat.' Mantos sucked in air, steadied his voice. 'Winger tell me de language was a real one. *Jerry jef* - dat's thanks. *Mon nob Mantos* - I luv Mantos. And was not no 'man' she say but '*mon*'. *Mon* mean me, mean I. *Mon return soon*. I comin back soon.

And he tell me de only thing dat *dat* could mean, especially dem three little fishbone on she face was dat Fatimi was from de same place dat most of us here come from, on de other side o dese three ocean. And dat she come from dere *direct*.

No storm didn blow her over - de mark on she shoulder tell him dat; if anyting it pull her up from down below. You see, dat mark was de mark of de name of a Inglish man name Luke Collinwood. Captin of a ship dem call de Zong.

Used to be a time you see when we wasn worth more dan de price of a cooking pot. And was like fish dem used to bring we here in de bottom of a boat across all dat water to sell. In a rockin darkness dat last more years dan I could count. And same like fish, some dead, some jump. Mos never reach dis side.

Dat Collinwood fella must ha watch de water, tink of all dem days an distance he mus travel and he decide was too much trouble. So what he do? He drop everybody overboard - de whole ship load - den he turn round an claim insurance. Dat chile - dat girl was one of em.

How come she reach here after all dis time? Well - I ask Winger de same ting, an I kin only tell you what he tell me, takin account o de fact dat dem say dat he was mad. Winger tell me dis. It got a road under de sea, a road o bones - like a cord o white - dat tie us to dat place cross dere where all de dust come from. An dat girl dat de English fella t'row over board, mebbe she been walkin all dis time. It jus take her a coupla hundred years to reach.

An den, an den we drive er back.

Dat's why I been preparin y'all sonny. Why all dese years I been warnin y'all about every drop o rain before it fall so y'all would stop lookin for yerself - for de real one when it come.'

As if it were a cue, a first hard sheet of rain sweeps in on them from the sea - like the sound of a million running feet on hollow ground. It douses them and then it passes abruptly.

'It reach,' he shouts pushing past the boy and heading for the track. 'C'mon fella, we have to go. Right now!'

He hears the boy's feet behind him as he allows gravity to take him down the track. His feet hits the sand just as the first hard wind like a giant invisible hand slams them against each other. They both fall over but Mantos does not stop. He stays lowered on the ground and begins moving in a rapid scuttle towards the houses. They cover most of the distance that way, pausing only to draw breath behind one of the larger rocks that stands between the houses and the sea.

'We stay up dere too long', he gasps. He turns his eyes up at the hill. The few trees that have stood around the clearing are no longer there. That first blast has shaved the cliff-top clean. 'Is a bad one - badder dan I thought. Is like night out here. C'mon, fella we almos home.'

'No!'

That stops the old man as if the boy has thrown a rope

around his neck and dragged him back. He suddenly feels frightened, cold. 'Now listen, sonny you -'

'I stay here.'

'You can't stay here!' In a terrible rush of anger he pushes his face into the boy's. '*Outside* here is trouble.'

'I stay, Mantos. I wan to stay.' Simon Coper has not raised his voice. Despite the wind, the awful noise about them, Mantos could hear his breathing.

'You can't.' The old man mumbles, shaping the words as he would to a child. 'You can't, my son. Ain't got no place out here for nobody. You see dat wind - dat little wind is nothing. Dat wind is just a test. You come to my place I -.'

'I stay.'

The youth is breathing faster now. In the murkiness, the old man can easily imagine him there against the stone, like some wounded thing that had simply lost the will to carry on.

'Okay - I believe you. I believe you didn kill dat girl. I didn like er anyway. Now, son -.'

'She was comin from de stand pipe. Bucket o water on she head. She see me. She start to run. Fraid o me. Fraid like hell. An den...' Something explodes at the back of the rock and destroys the rest of Simon Coper's words. Mantos flinches at the sound of splintering wood. A boat - the wind has tossed and crushed it like a leaf against the stone.

'C'mon, fella. I done tell you I believe you.'

'Don matter, it don't. Besides somebody have to meet de girl.'

Mantos forces a laugh. 'She won't be de same dis time. I tell you dat she change - not so? You could see it in dat wind. An - an perhaps she choose another place to land dis time.'

'Ain't got nothing you kin do to move me.'

Mantos knows that Simon Coper means it. And who could say that he would not have done the same? In fact didn't he do the same thing - once? Didn't he stay out there begging a storm to take him? And he truly believes that it had offered him what he could not find within himself or amongst his people - a deliverance of sorts. This boy, this boy whom he could never really love was already resigned to a fate that, as had been the case with him, he had assigned himself.

'Okay,' he grunts tiredly, foolishly - already scrambling up the slope. 'If you got any problem shout.'

Mantos does not hear the boy's reply.

He does not wait for it.

Ku-Kus:
Woman of Letters

These is the wuds of me, Ku-Kus Stanislaus which I decide to put on paper ever since I start to work in de Post Office. Yuh see, dat make me a woman of letters. Dat is what I does tell people who fast enough to ask me my bizness.

I been workin in de only post office in de Drylands for seven years an I is me own boss exceptin when de Inspector come an decide to ask me chupid question bout how I gettin on, an iffen I doin de govment work. I does invite im to walk round de parish an ask everybody iffen dem doesn get dem letter.

Letters. I have to say something bout letters for people who don't have de initiation in dem matters. Letters is a kind o hole in de door of people bizness. Letters does hold some of de sweetest secrets in de world. Iffen a pusson want to know what really happenin in other people life, jus read a letter from dem. An yunno, I don't always have to open dem

147

- even if we have we metodology which I kin tell y'all is a hi-falutin science an which I does resort to, as I tired tell Cyril, only in special circumstances of certain importance. But little later I goin come to dat.

Make it sufficient to say dat I is a expert. Dat I could tell by de colour of ah envelope an de quality of de paper who-an-who pretendin dat dem doin well in America, who-an-who really doin well an who-an-who only showin off. I know which of certain citizens in de Drylands here does hand letter to stranger to post back to dem so as dey could pretend dat dey have famly livin overseas. An I must say dat is something dem fresh little school girls specialise in when dem want to pretend dat is boyfriend dem never goin to have who writin dem. I have a very strong constitution but some of de wuds dem girl-chilren does write down in dem letters does shock all livin Christian decency out of me.

It have a coupla exceptions dat I make, specially ole Miss Tarka dat livin on she own who does post de same ten dollar note to sheself. She does come an get de letter an open it right in front of everybody to prove dat de wutless son she have in Trinidad sendin she money every month. She never know I mark it in de corner wit my Parker pen (wit de twenty carrot gold-plate cap and fine-writin tip) dat Cyril give me. An to prove de length and breadth of my considerateness, I never explode she cover an expose she.

But now an den I have to stop over a letter an consider how cantankerous de world is, how belligerent and ignorant some people does be, how stray-way an leggo-beast life does turn out sometimes.

Take dat young fella, bright as firefly backside who went away to study an left he girlfren tellin she to wait for im till he come back. Dat he only gone for three years an soon as he come back dey goin married. I happen to know dat he even went home to she fadder an mudder for she an de mother and fadder agree; an what happm? Well, a whole year dem writin one another like two people flingin paper across a room. Second year she slow down but he still flingin letter at she from cross dere in Swissalan like he blind heself deliberate o someting. De las letter she write im was in de third year an two weeks before he come back. She tell im dat she grow up. She is a big ooman now and she have more ideology in she head dan he.

I get upset, I get worry. A whole heap of quandary-an-confusion grip me an my Cyril didn like it cos he say de boderation make me stiff an unresponsive (he eddicated jus like me). I decide to go an talk to de girl an tell she to hold strain, dat is not only man dat does get tirsty but she mustn fling sheself at de nearest waterhole, cos dat fella really like she, so she better wait.

'When she ask you how you know so much o she business, what you goin tell she?' Cyril ask me. And yunno, I was so full up of indignant dat never cross me mind? Still, I nearly didn make dat letter go. I nearly write she back anomalusly an ask she what de arse she playin? How she could do something like dat? If is chupidness dat blind she? But Cyril wuds make me hold me houses. So I stamp de letter all de same an leave everyting to destination.

Is a long time now but I does still remember it an laugh, especially dem epistle dat dat fella uses to write. Pure poetry from start to finish. I never see nobody could explain luv so. Everytime he tell she he luv she, he have to explain what he mean. One time it was a train an she was de cosy compartment dat live inside he. Next time luv was a sky scraper and she was de light on de top. Is de first time I know skyscraper uses to have light on it. What make me laugh was when he say he was a rocket dat reach de soft center of she sky. I figure dat fella did have literary apprehension, same like me. But I dont tink dat my Cyril was goin to like dem kind of metaphorical employments from me. But still, with my kind of sensitiveness to de allurements of de written wuds, wuds like dat does reach me.

Make it sufficient to say dat de girl had she way, an last time I enquire I hear de fella recover an he overseas doin well. But I never forgive dat girl for writin all dem distressful letter to upset me.

Another ting dat does upset me is when malicious people start sendin letter overseas sayin who-an-who givin dem husban tabanca. I does even know when the man dem write to decide to pop up on she in secret. Is why I does look at a pusson sometimes and I does say in passin, 'Careful - trouble comin soon.' An I does leave dem to hold dat, so dat dem could make what dem want out of those few wuds. An de sensible ones does know eggzackly what I talkin bout. Is why people in dese parts believe dat me, Ku-Kus Stanislaus have de gifts of prophecy. An I would like to believe dat it have a little bit of verity in dat.

Still, all o dem tings is small potatoes compare to what I comin to now.

A coupla years ago, a letter pass through mih hands which, lookin back in retrospection, start off a whole heap of proclamating and declarating an man-hoovering between one hi-class family dat turn out to be worse dan a barrelful of mongoose inside a chicken coop. My Granny uses to say dat de higher up monkey climb de harder it bus it arse. Well, Missa Potray was one monkey dat fall an bus he tail so hard upto dis day he never recover proper and I have a special pleasure in declarin de part I play in it.

Like with most trouble in dese parts, de komess, start over property. Mih Granny uses to say dat property is a greedy man' word for murder. Is de only ting dat kin cancel out love an family; it does drive religion straight out of people head. My Granny say dat de only way to unnerstan where all of we come from is to study property. An believe me, dem is deep wuds dat have a lot of resonation.

Dem Potray uses was to live on de hill above we amongst all dem nice big house up dere. Everyting up dere white. Even de road dat take a pusson up dere white. Ain't got no whiter place dan Morne Perle Hill. Flowers don't grow no prettier nowhere else. Flowers dat refuse to push a root inside my little piece of land does flourish an rejoice up dere like if is dem native land: orchids, canna lily, jacaranda, trumpet flower, flamboyant. Is like if all de nicest tings was make to be up dere. Is like if dem flowers was tellin those of us below de same ting dat dem big house tellin we.

An dat Potray man walk like if he want de world to know dat he from up dere, with he nose point up as if it pickin-an-choosin which wind to smell. A pusson hear im talk an dem believe dat he stuff a coupla breadfruit in he mout. Was a tall man, greyin in mos parts exceptin in he attitude. Dat never change. Like de fact dat he hire every young girl dat was stupid o ignorant enough to do maid work for im, give dem chile an a coupla months after, he turn round an fire dem.

People tell me dat dem kind of behaviour is like a law of de land. Accusation and forgiveness and mortality don't have no relevance in dem kind of affairs. But I always tell dem dat I mus be born koky-eye o cross-eye, because I kin never look on dat kind of behaviour wit a toleratin eye.

But like I was sayin, a letter arrive one day and it change everytin for Missa Potray and in a litle way, for me. What pull mih attention to dat envelope was de fact dat de address was in typewrite. Is only govment people does type letter to people in dese parts, an when dat happen, experience tell me dat police soon to follow afterwards. But dat wasn no govment envelope cos it didn have no ON HER MAJESTY SO-AN-SO print outside. Besides, it was white and everybody know dat govment envelope was a dirty brown. So I tell meself dat it had to be some hi-falutin person jus showin off or something. De other ting was dat it smell o cigar. Dat tell me dat was some local big-shot fella with whiteman ways and pretenshiousness since white people don't hardly write no letter. All dem does do is send postcard to friend back home sayin how pretty everyting is an how de locals very nice an smilin think-you, along wit a few more compliment about de whiteness o we sand and de hotness o we hot sun.

Make it sufficient to say dat after usin my considerable brain-powers of reduction, dat letter had me more an more curious. After a little more thinkin I decide to use de power invested in me as postmistress who' first duty is to ensure the proper function of de postal system, an who retain de right (in exceptional circumstances of course), to closely inspect and dispose of, if necessary, any or all object or objects deemed prejudicial to de health an safety of staff, or public and/or de security of de state. Dat is what my little blue Post Office handbook say, and I does always consult dat before I do anyting abrasive. Is true dat I have to remind de trainees dat de govment send me sometimes, dat dis is NOT no encouragement to open people letter. I does tell dem dat experience staff like me know dat it have a delicate and important restriction between openin people letter (dat is illegal, I does tell dem) and inspectin dem closely which is a requirement of de job. An dat is exactly what I was constraint to do wit dis letter.

An I have to say here, dat it is because of dis close inspection dat I kin disclose here de wuds enclosed in dat letter, which I still remember verb-at-him and which follows as per say:-

> *John*
>
> *It is important that you find some way back here within the next week.*
>
> *Things have taken a turn for the worse with your grandmother and the stubborn old bitch wants to cede everything to Cecilia and her brood.*
>
> *That education of yours that I've busted my guts to pay for might do the family some good after all.*

I've done everything short of strangling that woman to make her change her mind. She blames me for all those problems she had before. She's made it clear she hates us.

Cecilia will not have the house or the property that is mine by right, even if I have to kill the lot myself.

Business, as you know, hasn't been good these last few years and that fool, Richard Kran, is now threatening me with repossession. They made him manager of the bank three months ago. I had to remind that potato that it was I who got him that bloody job.

Steve Potray

PS: I sent more detailed information through Margaret who said she was passing through Washington on her way to Canada. You could have at least confirmed you got it. I need some idea of what might be possible. After all you are the pharmacologist. Don't dissappoint me this time.

SP.

Well I read dat letter twice to mek sure I was really seein what I was hearin right. An with every one o dem sentence, mih heart rare up like a mad jackass an skin kuffum. In fact, was expire I thought I was goin to expire.

My Granny uses to say dat treachery is a nest o snake starin at a naked bottom. She teach me from small dat treachery is a treacherous ting an if dis wasn treachery I was holdin in my hand, I would ha gladly eat my heart.

I tek dat letter home but I didn read it out to my Cyril straight away. I decide to consider all de various opinions firs. It occur to me dat I kin go to Doctor Cornwall house an beg a telephone call to Ole Miss Potray an warn she dat she son plannin bastardly deeds against she. But I desist because everybody know how telephone does leak like strainer in dis place. How a pusson could be talkin delicate matters to a friend in Trinidad an a Chineeman somewhere in Nom Peng hearin all you business. So I decide to rule out dat opinion.

Thinkin back in retrospection, I sorry about two tings, I shouldn ha show my Cyril dat letter and I shouldn ha send it off. I don't blame Cyril but was he who persuade me after invokin all de reason why I had to send it: how was not my letter, how what was inside didn have no pertenance to me o he, how I might have commit a criminal defense by inspectin it too close, how dem kind o argument does happen inside family everyday an was only my 'magination dat put all dem notations to dem wuds.

Dat vex me for a week cos I didn like dem sinuations he was sinuatin about de motivations dat motivate me for ispectin de Potray letter.

An was a very hard an shockin look I give im when eggzackly two weeks after, de radio announce in de evenin Arbitraries dat Mrs Prunella Potray passed away quietly in she residence, leavin behind to mourn one son, a daughter an twelve granchilren. Was like somebody hit me in me heart. An a whole heap o grievance rise up in me chest an choke me, cos was smell dat I did smell a fart, which is what I tell Cyril. Cyril tell me dat it might be a co-incident. But when a couple days after, we hear dat Miss Cicely an three o she chilren was in hospital critically ill for inexplicit reasons, even Cyril face crease up like a pair of old trousers.

Now I is not a fast pusson by any sort of natural dispositioning. Nor is I de kind of pusson to meddle in people bizness without proper cause o motivation.

Till dis very day I don't have no way of explainin how come I wake up dat faithful Sunday mornin, put on me dress an mih hat, tek me hanbag an me little Bible (de King James De Luxe Edition with de real leather cover) an decide as usual to head for church. Cyril wasn comin dat mornin. I didn have noting on mih mind exceptin mih vexation wit im cos he tell me dat a dose o Pastor Greenway dat mornin was only goin to make he headache worse. So I start walkin as usual, saying mih usual 'G'mornin' to everybody I pass, ceptin certain envious an malicious citizens who' name have no relevance here, but who I will certainly make my notations about in de fullness of my time.

And yunno, de strangest of tings happen, cos I find my foot doin something dat I never know foot could do. Dem take over. Dem take me straight past dat church, straight past de post office and as if my hand was in agreement against me, I find meself wavin down Missa Cornwall minibus. Next ting I hear meself sayin, 'Mornin Missa Cornwall, I goin to de hospital.'

Make it sufficient to say, in a coupla hours I was up dere an after informin de nurse of my name an my status as Chief Postmistress and of certain connections an interests in Miss Cicely Potray, which I desisted from explainin, she allow me into de ward.

De woman was too weak even to look up at me when I call she name. A pretty girl she was, young as me an redder, wit a lot o dem spots on she hand dat you does find on fair skin people.

Lay down dere on she side like dat, she look like a empty flour-bag. De nurse inform me dat even if she was a little better now, Miss Cicely wouldn make no sense of what I say, so it didn make sense me sayin nothing.

I ask she what it was dat mek dem sick. She say was a mystery, cos after de doctor make he dognoses on dem he scratch he head an say he never seen nothing like it. Experience tell im dat it had to be some sort of affectation of de blood, but he had to carry out a lot o test to mek sure an dat could only get done in Trinidad cos he didn have de quipment here.

I went to see de chilren after. All of dem was sleepin same like dem mother exceptin de little girl who was not more dan five years old an pretty and helpless as a dolly. Was de sight o dat little girl chile dat make a coldness in me blood - an, yunno, something hard an bright like a knife sort of rise up an settle in mih head and durin all dat time it never leave me.

I leave dere almost in tears. I didn tell Cyril nothing when I reach home even when he grumble dat church finish long time an is now almost four o'clock an even if he did cook de rice, he didn know how to cook no chicken, so he didn have nothing to eat an dat make he headache even worse. I jus look at im, an praps he see in mih face what I did just see in dat hospital because he shut up straightaway.

Was den dat I learn someting about meself, someting dat I never even suspect: dat I is de kind o pusson who, once I start off something I have to persuade it till de very, very end. I realise dat is so I make. I realise dat was so my Granny make and I have de example of dat Laughin Tree in mih yard to prove it.

Make it sufficient to say dat de sight of dat woman an chilren in dat hospital never left me. Nights, I lay down by my Cyril, masticating about it in my head. It wouldn leave me. Was like a prickle stick to mih skin. I keep thinking of dat letter. I went through dem wuds over an over.

By dat time de funeral of de ole lady done happen. An I kin report dat it was a nice funeral, with de ole lady dress up like a bride, an all dem pretty an fancy wheats of flowers decorate she perfect an proper. I kin also report dat it had nuff wailin an gashin of teeth, includin Missa Potray imself. An I have to admit dat I did shed a coupla tears meself, an dem wasn from no crocodile either!

At dat funeral my interest was excited by de sight of a man standin near Missa Potray, who nose an eye never leave de top of dem trees dat surround we. Dat fella wasn makin no pretense of cryin. I even tink he look more frighten dan sad. Once o twice, he loosen the tie round he neck, look down at the coffin, an den he eye stray round as if dem tryin hard not to look at Missa Potray. But dem big brown eye o his was behavin de same way mi foot did behave dat Sunday mornin. Dem keep rollin up to Missa Potray face. Wasn't hard to know dat he was Missa Potray son, de one name John because de radio announce he arrival - two days after de bereavement - to de islan for de proceedings. An he was goin to be with us for three weeks.

Was also when I learn dat he was a farmer-cologist in America. My Cyril explain to me dat it didn have nothing agricultural bout dat word. A farmer-cologist, he say, is a pusson who know everyting bout medicine an mixture an what an what-not to make a body feel bad or better.

'Put it dis way,' my Cyril say, 'A farmer-cologist is a sort of hi-falutin obeahman. De difference is you study dat obeah overseas, an dem give you qualifications for it.'

What Cyril tell me bout farmercology and meeting dat girlchile, an de wuds of de nurse, specially bout affectation of de blood - all of it sort of start to come togedder in mih head, like dirty water comin from a lot o different place an settlin in one pool. An de more it happen, specially durin dem nights of thinkin an speculatin an restlessness, de surer I become of what-an-what did-an-didn take place. Only I didn have no way of explainin it. I didn have nothing to show nobody. Was like people who see jumbie in de night and 'fraid to talk bout it cos everybody goin tink dem mad or lyin. Is lonely I did feel. Is bad-temprance an discontented I did get. An my Cyril start lookin at me as if I was somebody else. He didn speak no more. He lef home early an come back late. All de time he look at me from under he eye as if he worry dat I goin do something bad to he. But it had no way dat I could shake dis ting off, cos was like a sickness dat had to run it course.

Is out of dis discontentment dat I start makin certain surrepetitious enquiries. In dis place people mouth always willin to run. If it had Olympics for mout-runnin, we'd ha been de topmost of all dem nations in de world. I sort of drop a wud here an dere 'bout Missa Potray and dem little girls dat he indispose, an soon I had all de name of who-an-who he leave wid chile, which he was never ever goin to own. When evenin come, I buy a coupla pound of sugar from de shop, a tin of Milo an I go to visit dem. All o dem know who I is, of course. An as soon as I start talkin bout Potray, de bitterness dat dem never realise dem had, sort of boil over an was so I learn a lot bout de man.

Dat he was de kind of person who whole being was a threat. Dem say dat Missa Potray never know how to ask for nothing. He just tek it when he want, an to hell wit what might happm after. An dem little girls wit all dem baby was livin proof of dat.

De girl I visit last was de one dat give me some proper hindsight. Is from she I learn dat Ole Miss Potray had special reason to hate im, even if he was she son. Cos he never tink twice about tiefing she papers an givin it to de bank so as he could get a lot of money to do funny business with - dat was when he was a young man - an she spend most of she life payin dat money back. Was de same way he manage to deprive Miss Cicely of a hi-falutin education overseas, cos de money de mother save for dat get tief an put away by him.

I ask she if she tink he had any feelins for he mother an dat mek she look at de sleepin baby on de bed an laugh. I ask she how dat baby happm. She didn answer, but a tightness come over all o she, an de woman-laugh she been throwin at me from de time I reach was gone. Dat was when she tell me. 'One of dem two behind it, Miss P.O. De Ole Ooman was strong as a cow. She never get sick beside de cold. An nobody will find out or do someting bout it. Yuh see how quick dem bury she?'

I agree dat de internment of de Ole Ooman was radder hasty. Dey didn leave much time for people to walk around de body an admire it. And den I ask she if she know de name of de girl who doin maid work for Missa Potray now. She say she know but dat dem wasn frien. I tell she dat, dat wasn no reason to hold back de name from me. I don't know why I ask dat question but lookin back in retrospection, it turn out to be de most important ting I pick up durin my excursioning durin all dat week - dat an de fact dat she tell me dat she thought dat the son, John Potray was even worse dan de fadder. Dat was all she was prepare to say.

I also take de trouble to write twenty five letters to my colleagues (some of dem I did train pussnally) all over de islan, includin a friend of mine at de general post office in town. Dem was glad to hear from me and deir reply come back pronto.

Around dat time news reach me dat Miss Cicely and de two boys was very weak but alright now but de little girl didn make it. Dat was when, over dinner, I look at Cryil straight in he eye an say, 'Poison.' He jump as if I hit im, and de spoon fall out he han. He was chewin and he mout stay open with de rice an peas starin out at me.

'You tell me farmer-cologist does cure, you didn tell me dat dem kin give you tings to kill you too. Dat it have tings dat dem kin give you dat don't leave no trace of itself after you gone. I figure I kin tell you how everyting dat happen did happen, exceptin de part dat Missa Potray son play in it. But he had ter, Cyrie. I sure o dat. He was de one dat give dat poison to he fadder.'

'He wasn on de islan, Feather. He come de day after.' Cyril swallow hard an say, 'All dese tings goin to your head. I-I don't know what happenin to you dese days, Feather. I..'.

'Well is from him de fadder get de substance. Dat letter say so plain. Dat letter ask de boy to come the week after he was s'pose to get it. It take four days for a letter to reach

America. Dat mean dat if he did come he would ha been here a coupla days before de ole lady pass way.'

Cyril look at me as if he want to cry, as if I was mortal ill, and he was tryin to placate me. 'P'raps he coulda post it, special delivery o someting?'

'Couldn a happm for me not to know. It don have no record of no correspondence or delivery, special o otherwise to Missa Potray from nobody in America; not here, not in de general post office in town, not in no other post office nowhere on dis island. Dat fella could ha send it with somebody who was comin, but I didn believe he do dat. Portray son fella had to be here before de say he was.'

'Ku-Kus..'.

'Cyril, I want you to help me find out how anybody kin travel from overseas, come to dis country an leave without nobody findin out.'

'Ku-Kus...'.

'I figure dat if was me I could take a plane to one o dem islands an - Cyril? What is de only ting dat kin bring a pusson here from overseas an nobody don't have to know, specially iffen dem don want nobody to know?'

'How you expect me to find out dat? You tink I have a police force in mih back pocket? You find I look like a govament? Eh? You want me to phone every airport in de West Indies to ask if dem had a fella name John Potray passin through? We have telephone? We could afford telephone? An when I phone dem airport an dem ask me who I is and where I from, what I goin tell dem? Dat I is Missa Sherlock Homes? Eh? You ever see me wearin khaki pants an funny hat? EH? You want me to walk in John Potray fadder house and inspect he passport? Ku-Kus, we is small people. You forget dat? I NOT DOIN NOTING.'

I was grinnin. I was sayin to meself, 'Ku-Kus is why you goin never exchange your Cyril for noting else. Cos even when he vex an talkin chupidness he does be givin you a answer.'

I put on mih lil-girl voice an rub he ears (the soft little part below) an I say, I say, 'Cyrie, Me, Ku-Kus Stanislaus, I luv yuh more dan money, better dan Julie mango. Yunno dat? Eh? Yunno dat.' He look at me suspicious and den he smile he pretty moonlight smile an go quiet like a baby. Dat does always work.

Same evenin I was in de house of the girl who workin as maid for Missa Potray. I talk to she gentle, an I give she de history of all dem girls who start off like she an end up in trouble with dat man. I didn mince mih wuds, I didn put mih mouth in boli. I put it to she straight. Den I ask she if she could read handwriting. She tell me she could read. I ask she to tell me de name of six country, she tell me eight. Bright girl, like all de rest who didn't escape unscratch. An den I tell she dat if she do what I ask she, I will pull certain rope dat is at my dispositioning for she to get a decent post office job. I even promise to train she meself.

Next evenin she come to de post office an pass me a piece o paper with she own handwriting. An I have to say she pass dat paper wit de gravity an decorum dat did speak very well for she as a future post mistress. I tell she thanks and to leave de Potray job straight away, don't even bother to go back, I say, cos there was a request for she to report to de General Post Office in St. George's forthwith, meanin of course de next day.

Dat piece o paper answer all mih question, even dem ones I didn ask. It lead me to reflections about people attitude to money an possessing. I don't have nothing against a lot o money even if it strike me dat money kin come like a pretty present wrap-up in a murderous dispossession. All my life I learn dat when I have too much I should share it wit dem who dont have none. That way too much is never enough. Dem Potrays see it de other way around.

It was with dese vexatiousness dat vex me up dat I siddown dat night and compose two letter. De one to Missa Potray, and to whomsoever else it may concern, went as per say:-

Mister Potray

You will see that I do not address you as 'dear', because there is nothing dear about yourself to me.

I have been and I still am a keen observer of the goings-on in your place of abode and your family. Or I should say, what remain of your family.

I have noted with the profoundest consternation and dismay, the passing of your mother and the incidents with Miss Cicely and her children. The passing of that little girl is what more than everything else God will not forgive you for. Me, I am only mortal and I am also a woman to who it has occurred that you are a man that specialise is destroying the female sex.

Numerous mysteries have come to light, the farthest from the least being the manner of the passing of your mother and that little girl. You did never know it, did you, that cognizant eyes have been fixed on you all this time.

I will not mention all your other immoralities and excesses purtaining to the nine-montly dispositioning of certain pure and virginal young girls who come to do maid work for you. I will ignore the complications (of a pregnant nature) that you cause them when the cocks come home to roast, by firing them afterwards. None of the above will I mention because I intend to stick to the point.

Furthermore, I will not explatiate on all the details of my knowledge except to line-out the following for your consideration as per say:-

I know that you write a certain letter to your son in America to come home and help you do your direful deeds against your family. You post that letter by hand through a certain Miss Margaret Rainer on her way to Canada in which (even if the contents have not made themselves available to me) you instructed your son to bring home to you certain substances of an innoxious nature.

You send another letter to your son asking him to come home straight away, in secret without nobody on this island knowing. It take me a considerable time (two days and one argument exactly) to figure out how a secret like dat could happen. But I done do so and now I can tell you that said son of yours did take a plane from Washington on the 12th October and travel to Miami from where he take another plane to Guyana on the same day. A boat from there to Union Island or Carriacou and then one that he hire from there to here is de only way of arriving in secret. The government will be notified by me of this loop in the hole of we immigration procedures in due course.

Mister John do his business with you and then he went back to America same way that he come. In all it take him four days.

When he come back for the funeral that you and he was responsible for, you all make everybody know, to make it look as if it was the first and only time he come.

I have to tell you, Mister Potray, that that is a starking, staring waste of good money in travel that doesn't go down well in the eyes of the Lord. Too much people does be needing money on this island to be wasting it on malicious, round-about trips like that, especially when all they coming to do is to poison their own family.

For instance I myself could do with a telephone. Money like that could buy me a hundred telephone, including the connection charge.

Make it sufficient to say that by the time you get this letter, Chief of Police, Nathaniel Godfrey Blinker - who study criminality and forensicks in England and who, as you know doesn't make no joke- will be notified by me.

After signin de letter anomalously, I seal de envelope and sit down to write de Chief of Police.

Make it sufficient to say dat a coupla days later, I was visited pusnally by de Chief of Police imself, along with a coupla people from some place dem call de See Eye Dee. An Cyril make sure dat I give im a bit of de credit for he contribution, which as de Chief of Police say, wasn't a lot to crow about. My Cyril answer back and say dat I is he ooman so both of we de same which nobody couldn argue with since he was right dere huggin me up in front of dem.

I was inform in due course dat dem catch de Potray boy tryin to jump de islan. An dat de police who was chasin de boat was constraint to pick im up from de sea.

Dat court case make a lot of fun an dramatics for everybody for two months.

Missa Potray bring a lot of defensive lawyer from Jamaica to cover he case. But he still got charge for crime I didn even know exist especially since he son decide to be de star witness. A coupla foreign doctor come from Englan an deter Ole Miss Potray body an dem conclude dat it was poison she was poison for true.

Den de Chief ask me how I come to know so much about criminalised detection, an what it was dat make me get superstitious in de first case, an iffen I ever thought of takin up dat kind of work as a serious vacation. I tell im I couldn answer im de firs part, for reasons of professional confidentiality, and dat a job with de See Eye Dee won't be necessary, think-yuh, since I did already apply to de Ministry of Home Affairs, of which de Prime Minister is de Pussnal Head, for the post of Clerk, an perhaps he kin put in a wud or three for me?

When dem left, my Cyril complain dat I didn tell im noting bout applyin for no new job and besides he didn unnerstan why I had ter. An seein as me an Cyril is always self-eddicatin one another, I was constraint to inform him dat Home Affairs is where every piece of govment correspondence does pass through.

An I have to say dat I didn like de way he look at me an shove dat spoonful of rice inside he mout at all, at all, at all.

Walking for My Mother

Old Hope turned out their children to watch her go. And it was both wonderful and frightening because the quiet in the air was all for her. All for her, the gifts, the utterances of pleasure, the sideways glances and sweat-rimmed smiles. Like they were seeing her properly for the first time.

Ken had gone into the bushes and brought back two glistening guavas. White and rare, they smelled of the last days of the Dry Season. Even the wrapping was unusual - a dasheen leaf, shaped like a heart and patterned with a web of purple veins. Her uncle placed the guavas on the table beside the bread they'd baked specially for her.

And Aunt Gigelle had brought her a boiled egg. She came swaying down the hill, balancing one in each palm as if they were the globes of life.

'Pretty peee-ople!' she sang, bending low and curving her very, very long fingers around her face and Liam's. 'One from Bucky and one from me. One fo Liam and one fo you.' And then, preciously, she placed them on the flowered tablecloth.

Uncle Ian had polished the new black patent leather shoes over and over till they shone like pools of water in the morning light while Gran Lil moved around her strangely. Her grandmother had taken off her headwrap and allowed her white mass of hair to uncoil and settle like a halo round her face.

Even her twin brother seemed amazed. Liam had promptly offered her the other egg. Every now and again he examined the brilliant white polyester shirt, passed the back of his hand against the dark-blue skirt and lifted the tip of the gold-striped, carmine tie.

They'd already begun preparing her. Aunty May had bathed her with the Cussons Imperial Leather soap they'd bought for the occasion. A new toothbrush that matched the ochre wrapping of the soap exactly and a little packet of Colgate toothpaste waited on the table while she ate in brand new socks and underwear. Occasionally her mother glanced at her and then at Liam, furtively.

Breakfast over, her mother dressed her. Her hands were trembling slightly.

Over the weeks she'd seen her mother take complete command of everything. Her moment had arrived and she'd slipped into it like a garment cut especially for her. She'd become strange and secretive and oddly compelling (a side of her Nella could barely believe existed), for her Mammy now ruled the yard with worry.

She had worried for a month about the money she didn't have, might never have, but had to have in order to buy the books and uniform. And gradually the yard began to worry too. She fretted for another week - her voice low, complaining, and very mildly accusing - till one Sunday, moody and fed up, Aunty May sent her off to take the good news to a friend of hers in some place named La Tante.

She'd returned home with fifteen dollars, which Mammy promptly took off her.

Gran Lil had also had enough and spent an entire day rummaging her memory for names of distant cousins, nephews, nieces and great aunts up north. She then sent the good news off through friends, by bus. Soon, crumpled packets began to arrive with pairs of socks and underwear; and bags with beautiful obscure books whose only purpose had been to sit on shelves near Bibles because they looked important. Sometimes they came wrapped on top of sacks of provision or between a couple of live chickens.

That was good but not enough, her mother fretted. What the chile needed most was money. 'Mooneeey.' Her voice drifted with the word, reluctant to let it go.

So over the evening meal, they helped each other recall ancient favours to old-time friends and once they'd settled on some names, they sent her off again, on her own. It was always on her own. Never, they warned, to mention money, or to remind them of the favours, just to pass the good news on.

Then one Sunday morning, with a long, momentous sigh, Mammy sat down on the steps, plunged her hand down her bosom and pulled out a handful of notes. She kept dipping and dropping fistfuls at her feet while they looked on fascinated.

'T'ree hundred, fifty wun dollars an',' she paused abruptly, her face rigid with anxiety. She beat a frantic tattoo on her chest, thrashed her skirt, stomped and heaved herself momentously before bringing her nose down to the stones in the yard. Finally, fingers poised as if to pick up a needle her mother retrieved something, grinned a large democratic grin and muttered fervently, victoriously, 'and one cents!' which raised a wave of laughter.

And then she left the money there for anyone to examine it, as if to say that her figure was, well, just that: hers! - a mere probability - and they, after counting it themselves, might just as easily come up with a different but equally legitimate sum.

Some stared at the notes, others prodded them with their fingers, or nudged them with a marvelling toe, or not uncommonly, brought their noses down to them. For nothing else on earth smelled as satisfying as three hundred EC dollars, and one cent.

With that money, her mother had bought her everything, including the breakfast of bacon, the bowl of steaming Quaker oats, and the Milo drink she hated but felt nonetheless obliged to drink because it was what eddicated children was s'pose ter have on their first day at any secondary school, anywhere in the world.

Now that she was about to set out, something tight and warm and frightened had settled in her stomach. It was partly due to the hush that seemed to settle over the valley. The neighbours had brought their children to the side of the road and had placed the younger ones directly in front of them, holding them there with both hands planted firmly on their shoulders.

The new bag of books dangling from her shoulders, and a few dollars stuffed down her pocket, she made her way down the track to the road. Aunty Paula walked in front, clearing the path of leaves and stones and whatever else she thought might make her trip and bruise her dignity.

'Yuh modder don't want you to take de bus from here.' Aunty May whispered.

She nodded - she would have nodded to anything. It was also Aunty May who told her that her Mammy, at the last minute, had decided not to come with her. 'She ain got nothin to put on,' she explained, and then she'd paused a while. 'An I not comin neider, so don't bodder look at me.'

'People gettin on as if I not comin back!' She muttered fretfully.

'You intend to?' Aunty May grinned cheerlessly at her.

'Is just a secondary school I going to, dat's all.'

The woman stopped wiping her face with her hand. Her lips were half-parted, her eyes cast down. 'You de first dis side of Old Hope Valley; in fact de first dis side of anywhere as far as I know to go to school in town. Once dem lil ones dere see dat you kin get to secandry, dey know dat dey kin get dere too, by de hook or by de crook. Dem tinkin mongst demself dat if Tin-Tin girl-chile kin do it, deir own chile kin do it too. Jealousy,' she chuckled loudly. 'Dat kind o jealousy is good.'

'People talk as if I deadin o someting.'

'Hush you mouth, you always complainin. Deadin me tail! I hope you not going ter talk like dat when you reach inside dem people hi-falutin, low-fartin school. You got to speak proper. Deadinggg - pronounce your G proper, hear? You got your handkerchief? Kay! Hold orrrn, Tin-Tin! Stop frettin at me! You can't see I fixin 'er?' She gasped and laughed and stepped away. 'Gwone chile, we give you broughtupsy, now go an get de eddication.'

'Where's Ma?'

'Never mind, she going ter be watching you. Everybody goin be watchin you.'

'And Liam? I want Liam to walk wit me, I want...'

'Never mind Liam. Liam goin ter be awright. Liam always goin ter be awright.'

Aunty May moved up close. She did a strange thing. She licked a finger and made a circle on her forehead. She then kissed the spot she'd marked.

'When you reach Cross Gap, you stop an wave, okay? Cos all o we goin be watchin over you.'

She knew straight away where they would be standing. Glory Cedar Hill was the only spot from which the whole snaking thread of asphalt could be seen all the way to Cross-Gap Junction.

'Walk, Nella. Walk tall an proudful like you never walk befo. Gwone gyul! Start walkin fo you modder.'

She lifted a querying face at her aunt, 'Walkin fo my...?' And then she understood. Aunty May turned and hurried back up the hill.

Miss Ticksy broke away from the crowd lining the roadside, wiped her hand on her dress and handed her a dollar bill. She stepped back and wiped her hand again. 'Tin-Tin is me friend,' she explained. 'An Nella is she daughter.' And she laughed a laugh that was loud enough for all of them.

She heard Missa Ram's dry voice, 'You break away, gyul! Look at my crosses! De lil gyul break away!' It was one of the rare times she had seen the old man off his donkey.

She took her time, feeling lost and not a little awkward. The new unfamiliar leather shoe made walking appropriately difficult. Shereen called her softly from the verge. She smiled back, shyly, uncomfortably, from the distance that her friend was placing her. The faces of her companions were all open and friendly. But they were not reaching out to her. They seemed to be taking her in with a new interest.

Half an hour later, still dazed, still drifting, she arrived at Cross-Gap Junction. Turning, she squinted up at Glory Cedar Hill.

Shapes they were, just shapes: her granny, Mammy and Aunty Paula and Aunty May and Shereen and Miss Ticksie and the rest of them. Shapes, dancing against the morning sky.

She thought she heard them singing. Or perhaps they were shouting something down to her. It all sounded like music anyway.

She waved back, walking as she waved, sensing with a sobering, abrupt sadness that she was also walking away from something else.

Ku-Kus:
Maculate Conceptualisation

It is with certain amounts of chagrin dat I, Ku-Kus Stanislaus feel constraint to chronicle what happm to me after I bring a certain Missa Potray to justice for killing he own mother.

I was Postmistress at de time, and I did earn meself some famousness for my part in dissolving the mystery. In fact, I even got praises from de govment.

And a coupla foreign journalist from Trinidad an Barbados travel all de way across de sea to question an interview me about my natral talents as a criminolgis.

I still upset with de Trinidad fella for takin mih picture when I wasn smilin. He didn give me no time to pose, or even to put on dem nice earring dat Cyril give me, or de pretty flower dress I buy fo one of mih friend chistening. Make it worse, I had de cold dat time an de camera ketch me in de middle of a sneeze. So I wasn please at all wit de potrayal of my portrait in de *Trinidad Gazette*.

Make it sufficient to say dat certain citizens who didn like to see me enjoying de fruits of my exploitations and my status as Chief Postmistress (I get promote after my adventures was advertise in de papers) dem begin to envy me. Dem get covetious. Dem get bad-minded. Dem turn long-mouth an ferocious. Dem even say dat I pretenshus and I tink I nice too much. Furthermore dem want to know what me an Cyril doin since he been with me so long an I not givin im no chilren. How come he don have anodder woman, pretty boy like he! Dat upset me cos dem talk as if I wasn pretty too. Like Cryil imself does say beauty is in de eye of de holder. An ent I dere for him to hold me?

But I is a very proudful woman so is ignore I decide to ignore de chattering of dem ignoramuses, specially since Cyril never pay no notice. Dat is how my Cyril is. He never notice chupidness. Was me who had to draw he attention to de fact dat from the time he buy the yellow Yahama bike with de special handle bar - from dat time, certain *citizens* start to watch me an he bad-eye. Is me who make him see that citizens used to come out in the road on Sundays just to watch me and he ridin down to the beach. An, yunno, Mrya son was brazen-face enough to ask me an Cyril how come we ridin to de beach when it take only a coupla minutes to walk 'cross dere. Was me who had to show Cyril dat more people start comin out to de side of de road to watch me an he from de time I start wearing de yellow dress an hat an shoe to match de Yahama.

I have ter admit dat I don't begrudge nobody de right to be envious of we, specially since dem never goin have de privilege of ownin deir very own, pussnal-an-private transportation, far less to wear a dress to match de colour of de gas tank. But I take exception to de fact dat certain citizens uses to call out to Cyril when we passin, an never say 'boo' to me. An dat Munro family was worse. Dem uses to say hello to he an pretend dat dem didn see me on de bike. But I soon find out was inferior motive dem did have. Was take dat dem decide to take my man from me.

Looking back in retrospection, I member a coupla people tryin to say someting to me. Dem keep askin me bout Cyril, how he was, an where he was, an how sure was I dat he was where I *say* he was. Did I or did I not know how far and fast a bike could travel, specially a yellow Yahama with special handlebar? Did I or did I not know dat after a while a fella does want mo dan food an lovin to stay content and stabilise? Did I or did I not know dat a lil bread in de oven was not a bad ting fo a fella and he ooman who livin togedder fo seven years? I tell dem dat when my fella want bread, is in de shop he does go and buy it, so I aint got nothing to worry bout. Dat make dem shut deir mouth an smile back kinda funny.

But one night, sudden so, I realise what dem been tryin to say to me. I was gettin ready to sleep when Cyril voice come across de sheet at me, 'Ku-Kus, how come we don't have no chilren after seven years, eh?'

Dat wake me up. Like somebody wrap a cold hand round mih heart becos it feel to me dat *dat* question carry a lot more question inside of it. So I think a while before I answer im, an when I answer im I say, 'Eh?'

'You didn hear me first time?'

'We never say we want no chilren, Cyrie, an we suttinly don't want none now, cos is only a coupla months since we buy de bike an...'

'I want one.'

'You never say so before.'

'I sayin so now, I..'

'You don jus pick up chilren like you pick mango off a tree yunno, Cyril.'

'I know.'

'You don...'

'I know - I still wan...'

'Me too,' I say an I cross me foot and shut me eye.

But I didn sleep. All de tings dem people say to me come back. I realise dat dem was warnin me dat someting was up with Cyril, or he was up to someting. Sudden so, I didn feel content no more. Fo me, happiness was like a plate of food dat had a lil bit of everyting in it. Now sudden so, I feel like if somebody was puttin dem hand in mih plate and takin my nicest piece of meat away.

'Chile!' I say to meself. 'What Cyril want wid chile? He tink dat chile come easy? Eh? Chile!' Chile jus didn sound like Cyril. In fact Cyril didn sound like Cyril.

I did want to wake im up an talk. I did want to wake im up an ask where dat question come from. Why now? How come it had to come now. Ent he know that some things does happen when dem suppose to happen and not before or after, eh? Is what extra I suppose to do apart from what everybody else does do, eh?

Next mornin, as soon as he open he mouth, I jump in first an say, 'Cos we not married, Cyril, dat's why!'

'Was de butter I was goin to ask you for,' he say, an den he look at me as if I jus teach im someting new. 'We have ter married fo dat?'

'Praps some people have ter,' I say. 'Before, before...' I was tremblin inside, cos my man never look so serious. He never watch at me so hard an different. 'My Granny used to tell me...'

'Let's married den.' He look at mih sort of hopeful an confuse an it strike me sudden so, dat it was not fed up he fed up with me. Wasn't useless he did feel I useless. I realise de problem wasn't even me or he.

'Who been talkin to you, Cyril?'

'Don ask me dat. You expect me to report de name an address of everybody I talk to, eh? What other man round here you know does report back every ting dat happm, to he ooman?'

Dat upset me cos Cyril never talk to me like dat before.

'You not all dem odder man round here, ' I say. 'You is who you is an I...'

'Ku-Kus - I ever tell you dat sometimes you does have too much mout? Dat you don't know when to hush an give a man a chance to tink?'

And so it was a couple of mornins after that, I try to stay out of he way. I didn give im no ba-bye kiss no more. An it didn look as if he notice. I was goin ter say dat he got quiet, but it wasn dat. My Cyrie was always a quiet fella, even when he vex. Was like de air around im get thicker, like he was wrap up in a big-big worry an he couldn shake it off. Mornins, when he walk out de door an mount de bike, was like he was bracing imself for a quarrel.

One ting I learn from my investigations of de Potray case was dat when you see a problem headin your way, you find out where it come from fast before it hit you. Dat is why when evenin come I acquire de habit of walkin along de road, and saying a sociable hello to citizens and standin up for a chat with de ones I get along with. And I kin report here dat it was not long before de name of a certain girl, Tilina Monro get mention a coupla times. Nothing direct or incriminalising, you see. Nothing I could say somebody say. But enough to point me in de right direction.

Most times Cyril was home in time fo de six o clock news. He like de six o clock news. He like to tell me which news is lie an which news cover up de real news. Now I notice dat he start reachin home after de news done finish.

It make me ask meself a question I never know I had in meself to ask. What reason I have in any case to believe dat Cyrie goin ter want to stay with me? It wasn as if I own nobody. It wasn as if nobody belong to nobody. An yunno, for de first time I start to look at meself in de mirror and not feel satisfy with what I see.

Is de first time it come to me dat it was a long time since I stop seein meself, or mih future without Cyril Wyferley. An dat really frighten me.

Still, dat was nothing compare to what I feel when one evenin I just happen to be talkin to Miss Anna-Joe who was a coupla houses from dem Monro. Sure nuff, I hear my Cyrie bike coming up de road. I see a young fella rush down from de Monro yard an wave im down. In two-twos was like de whole family occupy de road. Cyril stop de bike an he shake de fella hand and I could see dat dey know each other. Den de fadder an modder come down to de road, den dem big brodders. Dem laugh an slap Cyril on he shoulder an I could see dat he did an didn like it. Uh mean I never see im so confuse an happy at de same time. An den I hear de modder shout, *Tilly? Tilina! Come an say hello to Missa Cyril.* Dat was when de girl come out.

I know she well. She come to de post office sometimes but was like if I notice she for de first time. She was young an pretty, an very please with it. She say hello to Cyril an sort of look down at she foot an Cyrie look at de men as if he didn know what he suppose to do. One of de brodders say someting an laugh out loud an Cyrie laugh out loud same way, before he crank up de bike an leave dem.

Now when I find mesef in any kind of trouble, I always ask meself what my granny would do if she was me. An in two-twos de answer does come. But dis time I didn get no answer. Like she was tellin me, 'Feather you have ter find yuh way through this one by yuhself. I dead an gone arready an in any case I too ole fo dis kind of ting.'

Anyway, de way I figure it was dat I have three choice to choose from. I could siddong an cry an let dat pretty face young gyul have my Cyril. But I is not de siddong-an-cry-cry type o pusson. Or, I could go down de road, cuss up de girl crossways and lengthways and den threaten she with murder, but she had a lotta brodders to back she up and besides, mih status as post mistress delude me from dat possbility. I think about throwin it in Cyril face an makin a stink, but we never had dat kind of way of talking between we, an it might just add aggravation to de matters.

An den it had this other answer which hardly make no sense to me, cos it feel like it didn finish work itself out in mih head yet. All it need was a lil bit o time which I didn really have. Now people feel dat I does talk a lot an I does have opinion about everyting. But me Ku-Kus I have a quiet, watchin side dat does take over when tings start gettin hard an hurtful.

I begin to watch Cyril when I got home dat evenin. He was eating an I could see dat he was chewin on a worry more dan on de food. An it remind me of de first time I see im when he did come to evict me and my granny from we property. Was dem star-apple lip, an de moonlight smile dat did dazzle me dat time. I member how dry up fo wuds I become when he talk to me and how I couldn take mih eyes off he face cos he skin was so dark an smooth an pretty, like it have it own light coming out of it. Was like a mango tree dat send out dis one blossom an bear dis one mango when mango out a season. When it fall in your lap you jus know dat is someting better dan good luck; you jus know dat is a blessin.

I was glad he didn see me down de road watchin im with dem Monro people. I was glad I was there to see him though, cos dat is how I got to know where all this chile-talk an man-talk come from.

My Granny used ter say dat when a fella begin to shout dat he is man, dat is when he least sure of what he is. And to tell de truth I never see Cyril mongst men before. Was strange how he look, like he wasn happy fittin in. An I spose when a pusson don't feel comfortable mongst deir own kind, dey start lookin for someting to prove dat dey belong. My Cyril was alright till somebody make him doubt imself.

Dat was someting new I learn bout my man an I spose bout meself too, cos it strike me dat we don't have dat kind of problem. A woman is a woman and she know it from de time she become one.

Same like lil miss Tilina know she was. Same like I know she was not goin ter have Cyril. I could even bring meself to admit dat she was lil bit prettier dan me, but she didn know my Cyrie weaknesses an sweetnesses, and anyway I had mo intellectualness than she. Mebbe she really did like im an she must ha push 'er family to bring him close to she, but like I say, she wasn goin ter have my fella. An I have certain citizens to thank fo drawing my attention to de fact dat I really was ready to do a lil bit of bakin.

So dat night I clear me throat an tell Cyrie, 'I say, Cyril, You could remind me how conceptualisation does occur?'

'Teery o practise?' he say.

'It have a difference?' I ask.

Dat make im laugh.

An what happm after, happm.

Make it sufficient to say dat to dis day certain citizens believe I have a knowledge of Hi-science, dat being a very eddicated woman (deir wuds not mine), I must ha read Missa De Lawrence book. Some even think it might ha been a maculate conceptualisation, since dem couldn imagine butter meltin in me an Cyril mouth.

An when I break de news to him, even he was very shock. 'But how come, Feather? How come it happm only now an so soon?'

Well, I tell im what I tell im from de start. 'Cyril, like I say, it never did cross mih mind before.'

And There Were No Fireflies

For 'Jam'

The girl saw the shape of the older woman against the window when she slipped off the bike and in a sudden flush of pique she reached over, wrapped her arms around the boy and kissed him long and deep. Her aunt would get a good view of her tight behind and more, she hoped, since she had not bothered to arrange her skirt.

Joseph muttered something in her ear about tonight and the beach, and even if he often said that or something of the kind every time he dropped her off, she still laughed out loud with something of the annoyance that she carried so that the woman could hear her, understand that it was meant for her, and be suitably appalled.

The bike leapt away with a faked rage which, she thought, was very much like Joseph, the way he was with her, especially when he made her follow him to the beach. The sound of it bounced off the walls of the sleeping houses. And even if the Kawasaki had already run the full length of the street - its red brake lights a sudden glowing scar against the dark - she patted her hair, smoothed her butt, high-stepped beneath the single street light that faced her house and blew a final kiss not necessarily at him, but hopefully to aggravate the old woman more.

When Mariana turned to face the door, her smile was gone and so too was the woman. But she knew what to expect. The smile that came so easily with Lucy, Gordon, Sheila, Joseph Mayors and her friends was replaced now with a grimness, a tightness in the eyes that threatened a verbal reprisal to every conceivable warning she expected the aunt to throw at her.

Truth was, this woman tired her, irritated her in ways that no other person could ever do. And to make matters worse she realised over the past eight months, with the disgust of someone who had uncovered something nasty in her food, that she was ashamed of her. The shame had crept in on her like something secret and sat at the back of everything she said or did not say to Martha. It was why she always asked Joseph to stay across the street to wait for her. Why she never asked him in. Why, sometimes after school, she visited the houses of all her friends but never invited them home; why always, after the throbbing darkness of the night-club in the south, the hip-whipping wind-downs and soporific oozes on the dance floor, especially after she succumbed to Joseph's demanding way with her, she found a million ways to side-step his irritation and linger longer on the beach with him.

Just thinking of this was enough to inflame the thin skin of irritation with which she shouldered the door and marched into the house.

Martha - what kind of name was that? - was waiting for her in the middle of the cluttered living room, thin arms hanging down her sides, only the thumb of the left hand rubbing with little convulsions against the index finger. Those trembling hands were closed around a threat that would never materialise. Those hands had never struck her, not even as a child. And she remembered the innumerable times that Martha had explained to the group of uncomprehending country women who passed on Saturdays to ask for a cupful of iced water and fill her in on what was happening 'back home' that her sister's 'God-rest-er-soul' offspring was not and never would be hers to scold.

With some distaste, the girl thought of their laughter and their speech, the practised stridence they used so effectively to draw attention to their basketfuls of fish or fruit above the thundering traffic of the town. That stridence had - since her immersion in Joseph's world of parties, cars and light-skinned girls - become a pain. And at times she even found herself wishing that Martha never spoke at all.

'What time you call dis, Marie?'

'Don't know, don't care and my name is not Marie.'

'Where you been with dat boy again?'

'My business.'

Martha swallowed on a harsh intake of air. The hands convulsed and the girl flashed her eyes at them and then at the woman's face. She'd trampled with some pleasure on the head of every taboo that words or look or gesture allowed. But this - to look an adult in the face; her aunt, this woman with the high cheekbones and taut dark face, perpetually framed by an old head-wrap - to stare her down was the best of all her victories.

Martha shifted her lips, speaking with a resignation that had long become a habit, preparing to launch herself into a routine of recriminations that were as practised as a poem.

'Dat boy.'

'Like I say, is my flippin business!'

'He fadder's big-time lawyer. Same people like dat fadder o yours who...'

'So what!'

'He don wan de likes o you. Dat boy usin you. All o dem they usin you. You can't see dat? You mother..'.

'Me mother dead,' she threw back mockingly.
'Marie..'.
'My name is not Marie.'
The hands convulsed. Martha stared at her. 'Mariana,' she muttered, humbled more by the thought of what she might not have done, the thing she might have given or not given to what had been a free-laughing, easy-loving child, that had changed her into a hating, condemning presence over a matter of months.

'You sempteen,' she said tiredly and shifted her gaze. 'You got yuh studies to study. You got all yuh life in front o you. An besides you still a girl.'

The coolness with which Martha said this, the devastating certainty of those words used to leave her vexed for days. It was the one thing that, from the time this terrible and somehow edifying struggle began between them, Martha had not allowed herself to be bullied out of. It felt like the last hold that the woman had on her. And she'd finally worked out an answer.

'I got everything a woman got.'

If Martha was shaken by those words she showed it only in the sudden re-arranging of her head-tie. 'Still don make you one,' she muttered dryly. 'An will leave you with de same trouble dat dese people boy-chilren does leave poor-people girl chile with.'

Now the hands were perfectly still. 'I not strong enough for you. It tek me time to admit dat to meself. I didn prepare meself for de pusson you become. I didn expect it.' It came as an admission of defeat, softly spoken and flecked with sadness. 'You change an I pray to God dat don mean you spoil for good. Is all dat love.' She concluded finally, unhappily, 'It weaken me. But I got a cure for you. Yuh aunt Dalene will have to come.'

The girl laughed prettily. 'I don't know her, she don't know me. She's nothing.' That was how Sandra, Joseph's sister, would have said it. The way that girl could make a few harmless words just dribble with contempt was one of Sandra's abiding talents. She'd always envied that - that, along with her pride of bearing, her slim-fingered finickiness with food, with clothes, even with the colours she painted on her nails - which had to match her many shoes exactly. She had studied and adopted these, not without adding her own refinements of course. And Joseph seemed to appreciate her all the more for it along with the way she spoke now which had come easily, ever since she'd learnt to imagine each word as something soft on which to slowly chew.

'You more like her dan you tink,' Martha told her grimly. 'We'll see!' And with that she pulled the bedroom door before the girl could find a biting enough reply. It left her slightly dissatisfied. She was not accustomed to having her arguments end this way. It was she who closed her door and killed the quarrels mid-shout with an explosive finality that left the woman open-mouthed. The last word had always been hers.

She noticed straight away that Martha had been in her room. The towel she had dried herself with and left lying on the floor had been folded and hung up against the louvres to dry. The dresses she had flung on the bed in fits of indecisiveness were folded and stacked neatly on the pillow. The pairs of coloured strap-back shoes were laid like rows of multi-coloured fishes against the door. She dismissed the flood of guilt that washed over her and with a sudden flush of panic reached beneath the wardrobe. Her fingers rested on the softness of the packet she had placed there a few months ago and she sighed despite herself.

She straightened up and turned to the mirror to examine the person there: the face smooth and ovaloid and dimpled at the cheeks even when she was not smiling, which Joseph liked so much. Her eyes, catlike in the way they curved, large and lake-like in their darkness.

Beauty was the name that people called the way she looked

now, and until recently it had been something that was outside of her because she did not own it like she'd always owned her skin or limbs. It did not come from her, it was something that people kept on saying until she found a way to measure it: in the outspoken glances of the men that passed her on the streets; in the way a pair of eyes would pick her out amongst a crowd of girls and stay focused on her face. The way her passage through a group of boys would stop their conversation as if a sudden passing breeze had snatched their voices from their throats. And of course the value Joseph set on it, how he made her careful of the way she scratched her own skin because a mark there would upset him.

She was not like them. Not like Martha and that other crazy aunt of hers, which also meant that she had taken nothing from the mother who she did not miss because she had never known her. What she knew did not amount to much: an Assistant to a Head Nurse in the hospital, who'd fallen pregnant for the husband of the very same woman she was assisting and who one year after having her, had decided to die from something.

If anything, it was her father who explained her. She had his hair; not the straightness but the off-black bushiness whose tendency to curl she strenuously repulsed with generous swipes of Afro-Glo and Miss Unkurl. Hair which in this time of self-awareness was so mercifully unlike the recalcitrant pepper-seed of the aunt she'd come to loathe as much as she did the women who visited her on Saturdays.

Mariana stared at her nakedness in the mirror around whose frame she'd spent so many patient hours decorating and against which the weak blue light of the early morning came in through the window and etched a thin pellucid halo around the high backside, curved like a question mark; the legs unduly long which, amazingly, she had so hated once, and hips that flared beneath a waist so narrow she had to take in every skirt she bought. Her eyes paused, with an anxious, questioning reluctance, at the slight and living rise of stomach, that part of her that held so many terrors because of its benumbing possibilities. She remained still curious at what she saw, but stirred with a maturing appreciation of the power that this compact self had only recently acquired - almost of its own accord - over Joseph and the men who just two years ago would not have even known that she existed. And then still clothes-less, she dropped herself on the bed, reached beneath her pillow for the notepad and HB pencil and began to sketch with the same tense detachment with which she had just regarded herself in the mirror.

Sketching was something she simply did. It came to her as naturally as the desire for food or water. The impulse had always been there from as far back as she could remember, arriving at times completely unsolicited. She often likened it to a kind of water which, once stirred, flowed freely down her fingers, sometimes as pellucid as a sky, sometimes as dark as that of the well whose throat she'd peered down once on a school trip to the Drylands in the south. There, an old woman had told them, with a shrug that explained every outrage in the world, a girl or woman bereft of hope or love would sometimes dump a fresh-born child.

It was that dark water which she drew from now: a few lateral flashes of the wrist, a swift smudged arc capped by half a curlicue was Joseph crouched above her on the sand; and she, because no one could have seen her, was no more than a slight line, the jaggedness of a sensation, the bare suggestion of a presence so faint that it was hardly there, even less substantial than her aunt whose shape against the window she now scrubbed onto the paleness of the page with rapid, vengeful movements of the heel of her left hand.

Mariana worked until the perspiration beaded her hairline and ridged her nose. Their passage down her face onto the page did not distract her. Her wrist was tiring but there was one last thing she had to do.

She drew on what remained of the rancour of this night to give form to the aunt she did not know, the one Martha had so often threatened her with, especially these past months, and who for some reason had never cared enough to show her face.

Tonight was the first time she had threatened she would call the woman whom the girl referred to privately as Magdalene the Mad: a strange and wilful sister who had fled the lowlands and the canes to live on some godforsaken hill named Morne Riposte.

Dalene, Martha told her as a child, could make herself heard through storms from way up on the hillside where she lived, all the way down to Lower Old Hope 'as clean and clear as if she was speaking directly in a pusson ear.' Dalene was nourished by the violence of wind and rain and thunder, Martha boasted. She lit her fire with the lightening from the sky. Didn't it make a lot of sense then that she should chose a mountain, to be nearer to the elements?

Why, she wondered, would any woman even if she could talk across valleys and play god with lightning, choose to plant her house way up on the fringes of the forest above a wilderness of canes?

Exhausted she examined the damp paper and realised she'd made the woman tall, the hair rolling from her head like rope. All mouth. No roundness anywhere; all angles in the limbs. Barely a face. A rigid, living scream.

And as if it suddenly reminded her of something, she fumbled beneath the pillow for another pencil and just below the place where she had drawn Joseph and herself, she made a final stroke. Red and strong and certain because tonight, Joseph Mayors had hurt her.

With a short, dissatisfied sigh, she glared at her drawing of the demon aunt, abruptly tore the page away and crushed it in her fist.

On looking up she realised the room was flushed with daylight. The town was waking up, preparing to go about its business with the usual almighty crash and cough and shudder. She hesitated briefly over whether she should pull the curtains, and just as quickly decided against it.

Instead she drew the sheet up to her chin, shut her eyes and slept.

ooooooo

Voices pulled her out of sleep, or rather Martha's usual mutterings of bereaved resignation, which she had learnt a long time back her aunt reserved only for her country friends.

Strange then that when she lifted her head the house was filled with silence. Even the traffic of the town, subdued no doubt by the stewing midday heat, had settled down to a sullen deep-throated hum.

It was with this sense of slight disorientation that her eyes travelled around the walls of the room and took in with the usual distracted satisfaction, the things she had collected over time and pasted on the wall: the covers of two music albums, one by Third World - a Noah's Ark of rainbow-coloured creatures in a forest too perfect to be real; the other, a gleaming, long-necked girl standing on blue lettering that simply stated 'Bacharach'. The jagged-edged strip of colour snatched in a moment of reckless desire from an encyclopedia in the public library was meant to be part of an early painting by Cezanne.

Leaves. She had also collected those and pinned them up: an almond's for the improbability of its redness, an angel leaf, shaped like a heart and pale as sand for its lacelike delicacy. And finally a periwinkle that hadn't preserved well. Its blackened head was like an awkward full stop beneath the rows of sketches she had done herself.

The idle ease with which her eyes traversed the walls was shattered suddenly by the awareness that someone else was in the room. It manifested itself more as a sense of heat, and the gradual raising of the hairs on her skin moments before her eyes fell on the woman by the door.

The girl snatched the flimsy cotton sheet over her nakedness and pulled herself upright, a small cry escaping her.

'Dalene,' a voice came, a quiet voice, arriving it seemed from a long way off and wrapped in air.

'Dalene,' the woman said again, raising her voice as if she was not sure the girl had heard her. And still it remained soft, that voice, as her eyes travelled the length of the bed and settled on her face.

'Wha - what you doin in my room?' The girl's shout was loud enough to fill the house.

Martha entered running. She closed the door behind her, and leaned her weight against it. 'Is yuh aunt,' she said as if that explained everything. 'What all dis bawlin for?'

It might have been the way the light from the louvres fell on Martha's face but the set of her jaw seemed somehow firmer. And there was a clarity in her voice that hadn't been there before. Martha also held her stare. 'Dalene here, like I promise.'

There was not the usual apology in the way she stood or looked now, which the girl had come to believe was her due. And Mariana had the sudden, curious notion that the presence of the stranger had in some way fortified her.

The woman had not taken her eyes off her. She wasn't much to look at anyway. Another country woman with the same deferring eyes; the same quality of ease and anticipation in the face and a dark, unsettling muscularity, especially in the arms. She noticed too, the curious concentration of life they all seemed to have in the fingers. Fingers that never stayed still, that seemed to be forever testing the texture of some invisible bit of soil. It was a habit that returned to Martha whenever the girl's words reached her deep.

The woman was slightly taller than Martha. If there was anything that made her different it was her carelessness with clothes: a faded, flowered cotton dress, a pair of rubber slippers which was the nearest anyone could ever come to being barefoot and the inevitable pair of heavy silver bracelets passed down from God knows how many generations.

And this, this was the aunt that Martha had been threatening her with all this time. No wonder she had fled from people.

Still, it came as a mild shock to see her standing there. For if she had been real, it was only as stories had been to a child. Till now, despite Martha's invoking her these days, no longer as a woman of mystery but a way to kill her love for Joseph Mayors, the woman had occupied the same world as the trees that sang and the lions that quarrelled with spiders for territories and titles which, she realised as she grew older, populated a forest that resided only in the heads of older country women.

They were town people now and had been for as long as she could remember. There were no forests here. No sweet-talking, fast-thinking spider that tricked a murdering carnivore; no half-born or aborted child forever lost to the dark outside, knocking on a door for warmth or for some woman's womb to grow in.

She'd always got up to the thunder of traffic in the streets two rooms away.

And there were no fireflies, those insects that Martha said lit up a night like erratic flying candles and for which she'd kept her childhood curiosity. More so because she had heard enough from others to know that they existed.

That simple childhood curiosity had, over time, modified itself to become a puzzling desire to catch a firefly one day and preserve its fire on the wall.

The rest, including the stories of this aunt who could speak in a whisper and still be heard by others across valleys, who spoke to plants and made them grow; all of that, she had relegated to the backwaters of her mind, the place she reserved for legends, dreams and lies. Irrationally, stupidly, she felt a prick of disappointment.

The two seemed to be waiting for her to say something, their silence contributing to an uneasy feeling inside the girl. Martha's wordless siding with the woman, the stranger's direct stare made her shift with rising annoyance on the bed.

'I want to put my clothes on.'

Neither seemed to hear her. The town like a stray dog with its stink-sweet breath of rotting fruits, stewing drains and the subtle choke of cheap perfume and dry goods eased its presence in the room.

She decided that if their silence was meant to unnerve her, they were joking. They seemed to be waiting for her to say something, to explain herself. She could only guess at what Martha, with that perpetually appalled voice of hers, might have told the woman. She could only guess at the list of 'sins' she had spread out before this woman for her to gaze on and condemn. All in the name of family, an idea she hated as much as she did this aunt's interminable mewling.

For them, 'family' explained everything. It gave each of them the right to poke and stare at everybody else's intimacies, their embarrassments, their scandals. And worse, to dip their fingers into another person's victories as if it were a plate of food. The trail of commendations, awards, certificates of achievement had not stayed long enough with her to be hers. Martha had immediately made it theirs, for they were blood. And blood was brains. Was everything. And that aunt there, she glared at the woman contemptuously, badly dressed and as awkward as a stone, that too was blood.

'Get out!' she snapped, unable to hold back the ball of irritation in her throat. She was about to repeat the order when the woman's voice sliced across her words like the swing of a machete.

'Shut up. Get up! Go an bathe.' It stunned the girl. It was as if somebody had struck her on the ear. The woman stepped out of the relative darkness of the corner and now that the window-light was full on her, Mariana saw the shape of her face, how impossibly like Martha's it was, how dark the lips, how much rage a face could contain.

'Who-who de hell is you to...'

Again the voice lashed out and lopped off her words.

'Y'hear me!'

'I not...'

But something in the woman's demeanour suddenly dried her up.

'You!' She snarled, balling her fist against her waist. 'You - and you call yuhself a Safara!'

The outrage with which she said the name surprised the girl. This storming aunt did not invoke her 'sins' against her mother's memory the way Martha always did. If she knew of Joseph there was nothing in her tone to suggest it mattered. This woman's anger seemed to feed on one thing: that Mariana carried a name that she also had a claim to.

'She goin be takin you with her.' Martha cut in, sharply.

'I'm not going anywhere with that!'

She would never figure out how a hand could reach that far, or how the flat of a palm could hold the power of a thunder clap, or indeed how anyone could move across a room so fast. Joseph had slapped her once in front of his friends to prove that he could do it; it was like one of those pecks on the cheek that Susan practised on her friends compared to what now flushed her head with an explosive, dizzying darkness.

The face that peered down at her had not lost its distraction or the voice its throaty softness.

'Go an bathe,' it said.

She had barely recovered with the woman still hanging above her like the shadow of a tree, when another softness was thrust against her face. It was Martha's voice she heard this time.

'Three months pass an you don't use none o dese tings once. How come!'

Finding her fire again, the girl raised her head, perhaps to demand that they leave her alone, or simply to scream against this frightening twin assault. Instead she found herself checked by the sudden movement of the woman. Dalene had pushed her face close to hers. The girl could smell her hair, the musk of coconut and nutmeg oil. The woman's thumb shot out suddenly and brushed against her throat. It was a feather of a gesture, as fast as the flutter of an eyelid and just as gentle. But it seemed to bring a new grimness to Dalene's face.

Martha saw the expression and began to rub her fingers.

'Done happen,' Dalene breathed with a flat, chilling finality. Martha went through another transformation. She suddenly became herself again. She sighed that prolonged, throat-choked sigh the girl detested so much. Her eyes had gone dull and deep and sorrowful. Her hand reached up and brushed the head wrap, adjusted it and remained up there in a sort of aimless flutter.

'What you tink you hidin, chile? How long you tink you kin hide a ting like dat?' Dalene breathed in her face.

Unable to hold her eyes, the girl fixed the dried-out periwinkle on the wall.

'Go an bathe, I takin you with me.' This time it was neither an order nor a request; seemed somehow to require something other than agreement or resistance from the girl. And completely at a loss, Mariana began to cry.

That was how she found herself heading for some uncertain place named Morne Riposte, a suitcase packed with books, a couple of jeans, two large, ill-fitting dresses, ('becos ain' got no place to go up dere', Martha told her) and the little things she could not bear to leave behind: a ring fashioned from the shell of a gru-gru palm nut, three pebbles and a bit of pink glass she'd picked up from the beach and the only thing that Joseph had ever given her, a small bottle of gold-flecked paint for her fingernails which she'd later learnt had been his sister's.

And she'd forgotten her comb. And - on their way through the rising hills and quarries, past the tired-looking houses that leaned away from the road in much the same way as a person would do to protect their face from the dust and filth the passing bus threw up, through the smells of fermenting fruit and leeching soil, through the dark and cloying rank of vegetation that leaned over the road in a fluid, green confusion of otherworldly architectures - the fact that she did not have a comb was the final most embarrassing confirmation of her helplessness.

The long and tortuous journey was more potholes than road. It had imposed its own silence on the bus, packed with returning women laden with dry goods. Stern faced women with shoulders as wide as buildings or narrow as posts, who after the initial raucousness of the early part of the journey, had finally come to rest their eyes on thoughts that she could not even guess at. This was a side to them she had not seen before, these people who seemed to handle silence with the same ease they weaved their way through conversations.

She had noticed too, the way they responded to her aunt. Something to which she could not put a handle but which struck her as a curious kind of deference. They rarely looked Dalene in the eyes and it was with a galling sobriety that Mariana realised that she too had learnt to fear that gaze. For it was full of statements, one which - just like that awful order to 'go and bathe' - seemed always to hold a meaning that went beyond the words.

The driver was a thin young man with skin the colour of nutmegs. Throughout the journey he threw considering glances at her from the rear-view mirror and seemed indifferent to her hostility the times she caught him staring. When he stopped the bus to let them off, he pretended she was not there.

Dalene pulled a small sac from somewhere down her bosom and handed it to him. 'Fo your mother,' she said, the voice easy again and as distant as a wind. The man took it like someone receiving a secret. It occurred to the girl that it could not have been money that the demon aunt had 'paid' him. But whatever it was, the young man laid it preciously against the dashboard and thanked her.

'Your fourth cousin,' Dalene said to him, to which the driver nodded, his eyes rotating towards Marianna then quickly sliding off her face. In a fit of nervousness her hand crept up to her throat and stayed there, for it was something there, although she did not know exactly what it was, that had exposed her and had finally drawn the woman's wrath. Those fingers had simply passed there like an afterthought and had confirmed the most sickening of all the possibilities that she could think of, the one her mind had for more than seven weeks shut down itself against. And Dalene's soft-voiced, chilling confirmation - just three words - 'It done happen,' had made her suddenly a frightened child again. How could a finger brushed against the skin reveal so much?

'Is only Dalene could prevent de shame,' Martha told her, which for some reason had suddenly made school important again, had confirmed for her that she wanted all the things that it had promised her. School and perhaps, blood.

How Dalene could prevent the shame she had given little thought to. Her mind had simply refused to take her there. All she knew was that part of what was required was to accompany the woman.

With an odd mixture of belligerence and contrition, Martha had tried to prepare her for the journey. She had talked in that curious way that country women spoke sometimes, especially in the grip of some great feeling; in a language close to parables.

'She will take you up de ole stone road. De one dat climb like a crebeau snake over Old Hope Valley. Glory cedar trees, you can't miss dem cos dem rise up wid de road, an long before you come to dem, from down below you kin smell dem like a greetin. You kin smell de wind too, an de salt-an-freshness from de sea. An cane.' At that her eyes had darkened and that darkness had seemed to seep into her voice. 'It ain got no smell like cane, Marie. Ain't got no feelin like de feelin dat cane cause you eider. Is a man smell. A sad smell. De kind o smell dat is sadder dan de saddest times you never live. Ain't got no other smell kin full up you up an frighten you without you hardly knowin why. Just keep you eye on Dalene when you follow she up dat road.'

And on their parting, especially in Martha's kiss, she had felt something that went beyond forgiveness. Love, the woman had confessed, had weakened her and with the resting of Martha's lips on her forehead Mariana had got a sense of what she might have meant.

If Martha had prepared her for the climb, she had not told her what came before that: the stepping into greenness, into trees that seemed to have laid eternal claim to the earth on which they stood; the immersion in a world of wetness, stones and mud, and wading in air that flowed around the body like cold water. A humming that was not sound at all because it clung to the ears like damp cloth.

The demon aunt was no more than a shape before her, a shifting darkness that moved amongst the trees. Just once the woman stopped to dip beneath a bush and emerge with a machete in her hand. And then she had stepped back onto what could barely be called a path, hardly pausing to pick a leaf here, to chip a bit of bark there, to rummage at the foot of some tiny growing plant before up-rooting it. These she stuffed in a small plastic bag that had miraculously appeared around her wrist. They crossed a ravine and while she struggled after Dalene, a chill and rising anger gathering in her chest, the girl slipped and the bag of clothes spilt its guts out in the mud. The woman stopped but did not look back and seemed in some uncanny way, to know exactly when to take off again. Just when she was about to shout her defiance, to say that she was tired couldn't-anybody-see-that-she-was-doing-her best to keep up? they stepped out into day, the brightness of which struck her face like a sharp, unwelcoming slap.

'You dirty yuhself,' the woman said, glancing briefly at the mud-soaked canvas shoes and the scar of mud that ran down the front of her dress. Mariana clamped her lips and glared hatefully at the back that was abruptly turned on her.

The climb was an eternity. Dalene had begun to gather bits of dried wood which, after close inspection, she trimmed with a brisk flick of her machete and added to the ever-growing bundle on her head. The girl wondered if there was a limit to the size of the load this woman could carry. Dalene seemed indifferent to the weight as she swung up the hill, the old pair of rubber slippers at her heels.

She waded through the scents of flowering Glory cedar, like a drunk, sick and mud-stained, her footsteps fuelled by a hate that killed the tiredness and kept her climbing with a focused, tight-lipped determination; only dimly aware of the rising chill, the receding land below her, the total absence of anything human but themselves.

And in this landscape that was to her another country, all the things that Martha had told her about this woman who never tired, who walked as if no one else was there seemed more possible than ever and they began to feed her fears.

She remembered Martha's last embrace, the way the women in the bus did not look at them; the driver's eyes, slipping past her face like fish. Their face shut down, it seemed, on some knowledge that she would never have access to, and it occurred to her that in this landscape she could be made to disappear without raising a whisper. And she did not put it past the woman.

So focused was she on her rage she almost missed the house.

It was a tiny thing - a Janet house - with a narrow tin gutter running the length of the eaves and draining into a large yellow oil drum perched on a nest of stones to the left. It stooped on thick, very short concrete pillars a foot or so above the ground. From a distance, the house appeared legless because the lower part was hidden behind a flourishing fence of dasheen plants.

The bundle of wood rolled off the woman's head of its own volition and crashed onto the earth with a shattering finality. Dalene turned to the large drum, lifted a calabash which must have been floating on the water. She filled the container and began to wash her arms from the shoulders down. Finished, she turned to her feet, rubbing them vigorously on one of the nearby stones. And then on straightening up, she took the bag of clothes from the girl, handed her the calabash and muttered softly, 'bathe.'

She was too tired to retort that she would have done that anyway. That she was not like people who only washed their arms and feet after a sweaty half-day journey. Instead, her hand on her throat, she sat on a stone and stared bleakly at this new world that had been thrust on her.

Night was already hemming the tops of the hills. Below and from this distance, the canes were a darkening green in the strangely ash-grey light. The smell of Glory cedars reached her even here.

The occasional house sat almost unnecessarily amongst the spread of forest, like a speck of dirt on a clean, green garment. To her left, a mile or so further down the valley's slant, there was a huddle of hillside buildings, no more than a pale brown gash in the green like an untidy pile of leaves that somebody had forgotten to sweep up.

It occurred to her that she might spend the night out here. It would be her opening declaration of a war she'd begun and already won with Martha. One that sat on a carefully worked out conviction that nobody in the world could own her. That she was herself. Her life was hers, and that was that. Then she thought of the invisible mark residing somewhere (at the base of her throat) and suddenly felt fearful.

Dalene came out just then, her head-wrap gone, a loose shapeless dress of some indeterminate material thrown over her shoulders. She picked up the calabash at the feet of the girl and walked over to the drum.

It was more with disdain than curiosity that Mariana watched, from under hooded lids, Martha's older sister undress herself. And despite herself she became washed over with amazement as she took in the woman's length. For Dalene's body was clearly something to wonder at.

It was the darkest body she had ever seen, impossibly young, muscled and flared and curved; too strong, too straight, too assured of itself to be a girl's and clearly a thing that light loved. For what remained of it from the dying day fell and settled on her skin like dust.

The woman was throwing water on herself with careless, fluid movements of the arm, dipping over and over again always with the same rapid, flowing gesture that seemed somehow more like dance. Almost by instinct she reached for the paper and pencil that were not there.

The realisation of their absence left her feeling helpless, made worse by an odd conviction that no pencil on earth would ever translate this vision.

Perhaps, she told herself later, it was a sort of preparation for what greeted her when she entered the little house. She'd bathed with the same uncaring as the aunt, an odd sense of privacy and exposure out there in the yard that was not at all unpleasant. Night had fallen. That and the sudden chill that gripped the air had killed her desire to remain outside, had in fact driven her in, mildly shocked, for she realised that in the town she had never really seen night, not without the amber haze that always gave some shape to things. Here, even the valley below them had been swallowed by a dark and depthless void.

199

She was dimly aware that she had entered a room suffused with candlelight, her mind still on Martha or rather, the town she had been forced to leave.

Dalene was a moving darkness at the corner of her eye. The woman was rummaging inside the plastic bag she had carried slung on her wrist earlier on. On looking up, her face still tight with thought, Mariana halted, her eyes darting behind her to the darkness of the yard like a person reaching for some steadying familiar thing to brace against, because for a single, terrifying moment she'd completely lost a sense of where she was.

Dalene's small hall - she could not find the words for it - was like stepping into another world. An odd world of trees and rocks and skies, and above all, in the middle of everything and directly before her, a road. It took her a while before she could quieten her beating heart, before she realised it was a picture, a collage of some sort, the kind she used to do before she turned her hand to pencils.

She stared at the big, wide road, the light and shadows there, the converging lines retreating to a needlepoint in the distance that had, for a brief and terrifying moment, seemed so real, and then she turned her eyes on the woman, wondering in her astonishment if these nine candles were lit and placed around the small room just for her to see. If it was a sort of welcome or indeed Dalene's desire to further emphasise this apartness that she was, this distance which, without words or gesture seemed to be part of what defined her.

'You - you did that?' she quavered, realising the stupidity of the question even as she mouthed it.

Dalene paused to look her briefly in the face. She was less than three feet away and still the woman seemed to be peering from a distance. She did not answer.

The girl retreated inwardly, troubled somewhat that this - her first attempt to really say something to Dalene without being asked or forced to - seemed to mean nothing to the woman. She might have gone on and told her it was good, the picture, though that would not be the word. It would not account for or explain the thousands of books, the piles of magazines and newspapers that Dalene must have gone through to create this beautifully haphazard yet frightfully coherent world with photographs stripped of their skies and made to meld with other skies of other worlds. Trees that shot out of stones, and strips of empty air and grass sprouting flowers as heavy as hibiscus.

Her eyes returned to the road and lingered there - wide and dark and inviting where it began at the join between the floorboards and the wall, heading, beneath a jagged sky towards God-knows-where.

The rest of the room was like that - in a smaller way - lots of colour, shine and patterns, a white hand-knitted cloth covering the centre-table in the middle of the little living room, frilled with pink paper roses which looked almost real, two chairs made of bamboo. Nine gold-rimmed teacups that sat on a large matching tray on the top of a small mahogany table. Underneath the table a nest of speckled snails' shells were gathered in a pretty heap. And beside that, what appeared to be the tail of an animal - a donkey's perhaps - patterned with tiny white shells that sheened quietly in the muted light.

Pictures were pasted all around the walls. Hundreds of them. Unfamiliar reaches of rock, mountains, storms and deserts; wild and wrathful seas or, simply, not so much pictures as sensations, like the sudden flush of light through leaves, or drops of water making chains around a cobweb. Her eyes paused at a tree rooted amongst black rock, so tortured by wind it was crouched low to the earth, gnarled with the same consistency of the rocks amongst which it stood.

She could not help stealing glances at the woman, bent now over the coal-pot on a dresser built into the window.

'You, erm, you don't like people?' For she'd realised that in Dalene's landscape there was nothing that moved or lived.

Dalene reached for a pot, placed it on the fire and poured in several cupfuls of water.

'Yer have to decide tonight, cos what we eat from now depend on what you want.'

Dalene turned her back on the fire and, almost as if it were part of the same gesture, she retrieved the plastic bag of herbs and roots. The girl stared at her with luminous, puzzled eyes while the woman's meaning slowly dawned on her.

'De-decide?' she queried, softly, unsteadily. What decision could there be other than what had already been decided? From the moment she had left Martha, from the time Dalene had confirmed the thing she did not want to know, the decision had been made. That surely, was what Martha meant by ridding themselves of the shame? One did not choose an illness. An illness happened and when it did, a person simply did whatever was required to get better. But Dalene's statement, so flat, so clear, so void of feeling had raised a possibility that had not existed for her before and she felt as if a block of ice had settled in her stomach.

Dalene began laying the bits of plants on the table before her, placing them in two formations: one nearer the girl, the other to her right. Long-fingered, dark and sure, her hands quickly teased them into neat heaps. Mariana watched the movements of those hands, beautiful and flawless as her face. Hands that seemed to have an intelligence of their own, to possess a knowledge of these roots, these leaves, these slivers of red and brown and silver bark that were separate from the rest. And then, like an afterthought, with the same casualness with which she'd reached out and brushed her throat, Dalene slipped her hand into the bag and brought out what looked like several onions, only they were smaller and a glistening bluish cream in the lamplight. She laid all eight of them under her hand.

'These,' she gestured at the heap before the girl, 'kin make you strong an prepare you. Dem,' she glanced at the small pile on her right, 'will kill it by tomorrow.'

'Kill?' The girl stared at the arrangement mutely 'I...'

Dalene sighed a long and tired sigh. She drew one of the bamboo chairs and sat before the table. Mariana did the same, her eyes fixed timidly, like soft dark lakes on the woman's face. 'Kill - I- I don't like de way you put it,' she told her in a small voice.

Dalene's eyes settled on her. It was not unlike the way Martha used to stare at her, especially the times she returned from school with one of those certificates she'd won: a stillness and an absence of expression that said so much because so little was revealed. 'How else I mus put it?' Dalene asked. And it appeared as if the woman were really prepared to learn something from her.

'Is not a life. Not - not yet.'

Dalene reached beneath the table, her eyes still on Mariana. Her hand emerged with a bit of broken mirror. The girl realised that she must have placed it there just for this purpose. Dalene placed the mirror on the table as if it were a foreign object. She shifted the candle and held the glass up to the Mariana's face. Then, with the other hand she took one of the girl's fingers and placed it gently against the hollow of her throat. 'Dat not what it tellin de whole wide world,' she breathed. 'Dere, look dere. De pulse, dat's de baby tellin you it dere.' She then shifted her weight on the chair, and although it was a gentle movement, it seemed as if the whole house quaked.

'I-I dunno nothin 'bout dese tings. 'Sides, my school. I'm still a, still a.' She turned away, biting back the tears.

'I not tellin you to keep it,' Dalene sighed. 'I tellin you what I told your mother when she come to me with you. You was a pulse on she neck dat time too. I tell er a pusson don never get rid o tings like dat. Either way it stay wit you. An Chrissy was a big woman at de time, a Safara.'

'I'm a Safara too,' the girl snapped, fixing the woman hatefully. 'I didn't ask for the name. I could have had my father's name.'

The wine-dark lips sketched a smile. It suddenly struck the girl that Dalene might have tricked her into owning something she'd taught herself to be ashamed of, because till then, as far as she had always been concerned, that name had never represented her.

'I don't want it,' she said, surer of herself now.

'P'raps it don't want you either. A child does born knowin that you did never want it. And it carry dat knowledge in de blood. Vex till it want to burst. All de time. Without hardly knowin why. Ain got nobody in de whole wide world more full of vexation dan a child who come like dat.'

Dalene fixed considering eyes on her. 'I tell you what is true though. Ain't nobody kin love you more dan Martha gone and done, an suttinly not no little red-mouth, long-arse, pissin-tail boy who mek imself believe he is man by ridin poor-people girl-chile. Ain't got no amount o ungratefulness goin change dat. Martha love you like a curse. An a pusson got to be more full o spite dan dog have patience to turn an spit on dat.'

The woman's voice was still matter of fact but slightly louder. The most terrifying anger was the type that sat on stillness, like the only time she had ever seen Martha angry in the face of a teacher who had not given her the grade that she deserved, the type of anger that seemed to come from some place that was far and old and deep, that sat, it seemed, on the absorption of some lesson that somehow went beyond her. Dalene's was like that now, especially when she'd spoken about Joseph. And the woman's contempt surprised her.

Mariana was dimly aware of the wind outside rubbing itself against the house like some fretful, soft-furred beast. Dalene's eyes were still on her even though her mind seemed to have travelled off somewhere else. From time to time she passed a glance at the pot of boiling water, almost as if she were attentive to some question it was posing and for which only the girl could provide an answer.

Those glances did nothing to mollify Mariana's feeling of abandonment.

There was a smell in the air too, which at first she had put down to the smouldering fire or perhaps the heaps of herbs arranged before her on the table. But then the odour had become stronger and with it a heavy choking sensation that became a pressing weight against her chest.

And it suddenly threw her back to a bright Saturday morning in which she had been just as brightly dressed, walking into a government office on the Carenage. There, she had passed through several offices of the building she had watched every evening after school for days with the certificate of achievement she had won, hoping it would help her in a conversation she had rehearsed from the moment her awareness that she had a father had become a need. The man she had stood before had not got up from his desk to greet her. The office was exactly as she had imagined it with the large desk, the filing cabinets, the two telephones. What hadn't been part of it was a photograph of the man beside a grey-eyed, light-skinned woman and three children staring out bright and smiling at the world.

She'd stood before the desk and in a soft, unsteady voice had told him, 'I'm Mariana. Crissy - Christina Safara's daughter, and you are my, erm.' She'd stopped then, hearing her words as if they were issuing from another throat, for the idea worked over in her mind until it had become intimate, was not the same as the word and she found she could not say it. She realised that she had never used 'father' in relation to herself and at that moment it was like laying claim to a place she had never been to before. And the man was not helping her. The ease, the welcoming smile which she'd so many times imagined did not come from this tall, tight-lipped, staring stranger. Hostility or hate would have been better, she'd eventually decided, for they were things she would have recognised, not this flat-eyed, battened down indifference. This bone-chilling disdain.

She'd dropped the paper on the desk and ran out of the office into a day that had gone dull and oppressive. Had wandered home and wept, the periwinkle she had uprooted from between one of the cracks of the old colonial stone building already pulped and sappy in her hand.

'That smell,' she muttered tearfully as if it were the source of all her hurt.

'De canes,' Dalene told her. She sounded almost sad. 'De cold does make dem sweat.' And almost as an afterthought she added, 'Is de time o de fireflies. Martha say you never seen a firefly?' With that Dalene got up, unwound a string from around a nail beside the shutters that faced the valley and flung it open. She held it there in a wordless invitation.

Mariana dragged herself off the chair. The smell hit her in the face like a dirty towel, and she staggered back slightly, clamping her jaws down on the sickness that welled up in her chest.

And there it was just as Martha had told her. A glowing, shifting, twinkling mist of lights stippling the void below them. And for the first time in that day her face softened, something between a grimace and a smile, between illness and elation and forgetting herself, she turned to the woman, childish, amazed.

'Fireflies I, I would like to catch one.'

'Ketch one?' Dalene's voice came back surprised. 'Fo what?'

'Fo me,' she answered simply.

'Never worth de trouble,' Dalene's chuckle was a soft cough. 'You ketch one an it die. An when it die, de light does die. Besides...' Her voice was an oddly hollow sound as she turned away from the window.

'Besides?' The girl shifted questioning eyes on her.

She turned to face Mariana, her demeanour tight and contemplative; and for the first time the girl detected a reluctance in her tone. 'You sure you wan to hear?'

Mariana nodded.

Dalene's hand fluttered above her head, a quick unconscious gesture that was also one of Martha's. 'People dis part o de world believe dat dem firefly is not jus little tings dat fly bout here, come night time. Is de spirit o all de unborn dat visit us, to ketch a glimpse of dis world dem never got to see'.

The girl looked at her uneasily.

There was a new depth to her voice now. It seemed somehow to match the awful smell that came up to oppress them. 'Y'see, Mariana Safara, dat's why dem carry dat light, so as to see jus a little bit of dis worl. Just enough to mek dem decide whether to try to come again o not.

Y'see, it used to have a time amongst dem cane down dere when a woman might decide she didn want no chile o hers to inherit dat abomination. And I don see how I kin blame er. It had Safaras amongst dem too. What trouble me sometimes is if all o dem did decide to do de same, me an you wouldn be standin here. We'd ha been two firefly. Besides...'

'I don' want to hear no more.'

'You ask me,' Dalene told her flatly and returned to the pot.

Joseph would laugh that short derisive laugh of his if he could see her now. Here with an aunt she'd barely admitted to herself, far less to him. Joseph of the rough-gentle ways, whose spirit fed on fun, who rarely listened long enough to really hear what people said, whom she sometimes surprised and irritated with the little things she showed him like the colours on a hillside, the patterns on a seashell, the curve of a road. She wondered where he was now. Perhaps on a beach somewhere with his friends, not staring at the sea, not listening to its cough and thunder but trying to shut it out with the music of Credence Clear Water Revival or Joe Cocker and his Mad Dogs.

'I believe he spite me,' she said suddenly, drawing from a well of bitterness that rushed up and surprised her. And with that simple statement, as if something had been unplugged in her, came the flood of little humiliations, the tiny, teasing resentments, the accepting without wanting. All the things he'd said and did not say, did and did not do, which she hadn't realised registered. What it had really required of her just to be the way he wanted. The fact that her presence here with Dalene might have been the result of what Martha called her 'foolishness' took nothing away from the conviction or the bitterness she felt, the sense of having been betrayed.

It was a bitterness that Dalene echoed softly, pre-occupied now with laying out two plates of fried fish, bread and butter. She'd cleared the table of the plants just as quickly as she'd laid it out.

'Man is a hoe,' she grumbled, pausing to look at the girl and then gently to place the plate before her. 'He always leave a mark. Eat and sleep. We'll both be surer in de mornin.'